AF373822

Romancing the Gorgon

Tallie Rose

Copyright © Tallie Rose 20223
All rights reserved. No part of this book may be used or reproduced in any manner without prior written permission from the copyright owner, except for brief excerpts for review or summary.

Cover art by Drew Montgomery

www.tallierose.com
Twitter: _tallierose
Instagram: _tallierose

To everyone who dared to be a little bit different and all the people who loved them for it.

-CHAPTER ONE-

THE BROWN, RATTLING remains of leaves stirred above Lettie's head, a reminder that winter would soon be there, that winds would turn the surface of the lake, and soon the last of the straggling tourists would be gone for the season. Lettie usually loved this time of year. Lilac Lake was hardly a tourist destination, but summer and spring brought in strange faces and fuller streets. She usually liked the winter, when everything was quiet, when she knew everyone, when the town was just hers.

Today Lilac Lake felt like a dud. Like no matter how hard she tried it would not open to her, let her sink her teeth into the deep marrow at its core. Or maybe she was just in a bad mood, maybe she just knew the world class coffee at Hershel's Diner was just Folgers and that the underside of the pier was thick with chewed gum. Mostly it was that she'd been outbid—again—by an out-of-town investor.

Though she still had her grandmother's lodge in some ways; she still worked each day, and greeted the guests, and ordered the linens, and did all the things a manager would do. But she'd thought it would be *hers*, that she would really and truly own a piece of the town, instead her grandmother had died and her will had made no mention of the Stone and Sorcery Lodge she owned half of.

So, without the Lodge in her name, Lettie wanted to grab every piece of the town she should get and hold on to it, make sure nothing changed, because she knew in five years—or ten or maybe even twenty—but she knew eventually more people would flock to the town, it would grow and change and become something she didn't recognize.

And then, she worried something even worse would happen. The appeal of the town would wear off, the tourists would thin, all the investors grabbing land like Halloween candy would lose interest, and the town would become one of those sad places you drove through and felt sorry for.

Lately, Lettie worried a lot.

Deep inside her, pushed down, her magic twisted, but she tried to ignore it. No good came of being a witch, at least not for Lettie, though others thrived on it. But Lettie did not do magic, not even a parlor trick. It had been a long time since she'd given up on her magic, and though it often tried to make itself known she never gave it a chance.

She kicked one of the pebbles lining the lake's shore and crossed her denim-clad arms across her chest. She shouldn't be so morose, she had a meeting with the town lawyer, Albert Hillchamp, in an hour and she had an idea of what he would say. Or at least a hope. The only flicker of it she'd had since her grandmother, Hattie, had passed.

Her grandmother's best friend, Everly Hart, had died a month ago. She'd been ready for it at the end, missing her friend, her husband. She'd been ready to go and that had made it easier for everyone who had loved her.

Grinding her teeth, Lettie tried to push away her ideas about her meeting with Hillchamp and not let hope settle into her mind, a dream too good to come true. She couldn't think about Stone and Sorcery Lodge and all the memories that came with it because her expectations would get too high and just like everything else, they were liable to come crashing down around her.

"Fuck." she muttered, running a hand through her strawberry blonde hair. "Get it together, Katz." Her magic sparked again at her fingertips, more active than it usually was, and she balled her hands into fists extinguishing it. It had been trying to break free all week, like it knew something she didn't.

She really was a ball of nerves, both excited and terrified at the thought of her meeting with the lawyer. To calm herself, she looked towards the center of the lake, the magical heart of the town, and heard the whisper in the wind.

There were plenty of places in the world where Supernaturals gathered, where magic flowed, and anything seemed possible. But the people of Lilac Lake had held their secret close until, like all things, it had eventually flowed through their fingers and into the world.

There were cities where fae roamed, resort towns where witches and shifters rubbed elbows, but few places where the most feared of the Supernaturals walked—the ones that history had seen as demons, the sirens and gorgons and banshees.

For most of the town's history they had held that secret close, but then the journalists had come, the photographers and the newscasters. Sure, it had been before Lettie was born, but it had been her grandmother's favorite story. Probably because it was about her and Everly, the witch and the gorgon, and the namesakes of the Lodge.

The story—and the way the secret had gotten out—said that Everly had turned Hattie to stone. Her grandmother would chuckle as she told them how it was supposed to be funny, but the art judges at the county fair hadn't thought so. The story had snowballed after that until everyone knew about gorgons, sirens, and banshees, and the little town where they lived.

The mayor had issued a sanction against the two of them and they'd laughed at that too, as they did interviews and radio spots until they had enough money to buy the land where the Lodge now stood.

And at some point, everyone had forgotten how mad they were. Everly and Hattie had brought in tourism, and the increase in money had come with a change of heart for the townsfolk.

Now they were both gone, the two old ladies who had been the center point of Lettie's universe. And she didn't know how to see Hillchamp, how to watch Everly's possessions split up and called assets. She definitely didn't know what she would do if the Lodge, once again, didn't go to her.

It had been hard with her grandmother, but now the situation had gotten dire. Though the Lodge was still open, the women had gotten too old to properly care for it and despite Lettie's best intentions she could only do so much without owning it. The Lodge was overgrown, the paint was peeling, and the small cabins at the lake's shore that had once been an all-girl's summer camp were falling apart, full of raccoons and debris.

"Fuck," she repeated and turned her back on the lake. Usually, Lettie was not a glass half empty kind of woman. She was bright and cheerful and wore blazers in shades of colors her grandmother had described as garish.

At least she had.

Lettie left the lake behind and headed towards Main Street. The town was quiet, too late to grab a cup of coffee, too early for lunch, and not the season for brunch. She pulled out her phone as she turned onto the main strip of town and scrolled through messages until she found a string of texts between her and her best friend Daphne.

She started to type.

Hey, are you

"Watch out!"

Lettie's phone tumbled from her fingers, skittering across the pavement. The woman she'd nearly steamrolled bent down at the same time she did, and she realized what was happening, but she realized too late, as they crashed into each other, and the woman fell right onto her ass.

Then she looked up. And Lettie wished the pavement beneath her feet would open up and swallow her whole. That she'd turn into goo and sink through the cracks in the pavement. Anything but looking down into the wide green eyes of Chandler Hart.

"First your brother and now you. Katz everywhere." Chandler pushed herself up from the sidewalk and brushed off her jeans.

Suddenly Lettie was seventeen again, crying into her pillow. "Why are you here?" The words spilled from her lips seemingly before they passed through her brain. She could feel the blush that spread across her cheeks. Chandler's grandma had died, her will reading was today. Of course, she was here. "I mean—It's good to see you."

"Is it?" Chandler cocked her head to the side. Her mess of black curls was shorter than it had been when they were teenagers, she'd gotten her septum pierced and several black tattoos—of literal snakes—made their way up her arms. Apparently, she'd really embraced the gorgon in the big city thing.

Was it good to see her? Lettie shrugged. "It's what people say."

"Yeah, okay." Chandler laughed. "Anyway, I'm gonna go."

"Yeah." Lettie watched her take a step. Then another. "Hey Chandler, I'm sorry about your grandmother. She was…"

Chandler's shoulders tightened, but she didn't turn, just waved a dismissive hand towards Lettie. "It's whatever. She liked you better anyway."

This time Lettie let her go. She picked her phone from the sidewalk and put it back in her pocket. Chandler was back in town. Lettie knew she came back sometime, but she'd always avoided her. And that was fine, really it was nothing. When Chandler had left Lettie had spent a week crying and then she'd moved on. She'd found other things to occupy her time, she'd had senior year, girls who hadn't spent the better part of their life ignoring her. She'd had much more to do than worry about Chandler Hart.

And eventually she'd mostly stopped thinking about Chandler at all. She was a part of the past. Plenty of people moved out of Lilac Lake, even Lettie had thought about it a time or two. She took a breath and headed into the closest door.

"Well, shit. I thought that was you out there," Margery Price said as the bell above the coffee shop door rang. "Can you believe she's here? Some nerve coming back. Couldn't bother when her own grandma was dying and then last night, screaming at your brother like that."

"She screamed at Lorne?" Lettie wished she had kept walking. She would have if she had known Margery was working. It wasn't that she disliked Margery, it was just that she needed a moment to think and that was not something easily accomplished near someone as talkative as Margery.

"Well, that's what I heard. I wasn't there. Been avoiding him, you know." Unfortunately, Lettie did know, despite her best efforts, the ups and downs of Margery and Lorne. She let Margery keep talking—thought she didn't have much of a choice—while she browsed the stainless steel mugs. "But something happened at The Three Sisters, I don't know. I guess he made a joke or something. Said something about the funeral and she just started yelling. I don't know. I don't like to gossip."

"Of course not."

"Though I heard that there was a commotion at the will reading yesterday. Her mama left in tears—"

"The will reading was yesterday?" Lettie snatched her phone from her pocket and pulled up her emails. Her appointment was definitely today. It was definitely today in ten minutes. She frowned as she said her goodbyes to Margery. She'd made a lot of assumptions when Hillchamp had asked her to come by.

She rushed the three blocks to Hillchamp's office, a converted house off Sweetwater Street, trying and failing not to let her worries get the better of her. Then she came around a corner and seriously considered turning around. Chandler was standing on the porch, scowling down at her own phone.

-CHAPTER TWO-

LETTIE SLOWED HER pace, though she wasn't sure what she was hoping for. But she didn't want to talk to Chandler, she didn't have anything to say. What was there even to talk about? *Remember how I thought we were falling in love for a month after my junior year of high school and then everything went to shit, and you left forever?*

And she really wasn't holding onto it. She just didn't want to talk to Chandler either. She liked the town better when she wasn't running into her high school ex twice in one day.

Something scurried in the bushes outside the lawyer's office, and Chandler looked down without noticing Lettie. The scowl melted from her face, and she reached over, plucking up a snake. It wound around her wrist, and she brought it to eye level.

Lettie was just a witch, and not a particularly powerful one. And sometimes, just for moments, she was a little jealous of the other supernaturals. Except she knew gorgons got the shit end of it because it was most definitely illegal to turn someone into stone and charming snakes was a cool trick but had few real-world applications. That was the plight of most of the magical inhabitants of Lilac Lake—they had magic, but it was unusable, at least legally speaking.

Chandler let the snake slither off her arm and back down into the shrubbery, and her gaze caught on Lettie. She frowned. "What the hell are you doing here?"

Lettie walked up the porch steps. "Hillchamp said he wanted to meet with me about your grandma's will."

Chandler leaned against the porch railing and chuckled, low and ominous. "Oh, that's rich. But like I said, she always liked you better."

"That's not fair, Chandler. You weren't here. Besides, you have no idea what Hillchamp is going to say."

"Oh, don't I?" She raised a single eyebrow. Her grandma Everly had been able to do the same thing.

Lettie almost started to argue, she had opened her mouth to do just that when Hillchamp appeared in the doorway. "Ms. Katz, Ms. Hart, why are you waiting on the porch? Come on in, take a seat!" He ushered them inside and led them to his office.

Everything was dark wood and dark green, like she'd been plunged into some forest. Hillchamp sat behind his desk, but Lettie kept standing. He was a pleasant man, always smiling, always ready to help, but Lettie found him a bit…oily. Smiling too wide, too eager to please. And to be honest, not very good at his job.

He smiled at the two of them from behind his mahogany desk and cleared his throat. "Ladies, why don't you take a seat."

Lettie glanced at Chandler to find the gorgon staring at her.

"Ladies…" Hillchamp repeated.

With a scowl, Chandler sat, and Lettie did the same.

"Gonna turn me into stone?" Lettie asked, raising an eyebrow. It was a low blow, but the way Chandler kept looking at her, like she was the one who had done something wrong, struck a nerve. This was her town, and she couldn't wait for Chandler to be out of it again.

"Screw you." Chandler shifted in her chair.

"Ladies!" Hillchamp snapped his fingers. "Now, you both stop that right now or I'll bring your mamas to this meeting." He waited a beat. "Thank you." He rested his arms on her desk and leaned forward. "The reason I asked you here was to hopefully avoid a repeat of what happened at the Summer Festival all those years ago."

Lettie looked down at her hands, remembering the way they had vibrated over a decade ago. It was the most magic she'd ever done, and it had taken years to live the reputation down.

"It was an accident," Chandler said, her voice sheepish and Lettie was glad to know Chandler was just as embarrassed about that day as she was.

"Yes, but it was quite a big explosion. Town square still isn't perfectly level." Hillchamp straightened the papers on his desk and pulled one to the top. "Moving on, and I'll cut right to the chase, Everly Hart left the Stone and Sorcery Lodge to both of you ladies in equal shares."

The Stone and Sorcery Lodge was hers? Lettie's magic shot around her insides like it was the Fourth of July and for once she didn't bother to fight against it. She'd hoped this was why he'd emailed, but she hadn't let herself truly believe, hadn't even mentioned the meeting to her family.

"No." Chandler braced her arms on the chair and started to stand then plopped back down. "Come on, Mr. Hillchamp. I don't want the lodge."

"Well, I do!" Lettie said, straining her neck to see exactly what the paper said. "I'll take her shares too."

"Well, I would have to look into that because—"

"No way." Chandler stood and walked over to the window; her hands shoved into the pockets of her jeans.

"You just said you didn't want it." Lettie couldn't believe this. Chandler didn't care one bit about Lilac Lake or the Lodge. She couldn't expect Lettie to pay her for it.

"So, you should have it, golden girl?"

"Well…" Hillchamp glanced between the two of them with the look of a man ready to duck for cover under his desk. "It says here that if either party wants to sell within six months, they must pass ownership to the other party. Now, Chandler, you don't know much about what's going on around here, but the town's being bought up. I'm sure your grandmother wanted to avoid that."

"Is there any way around it?" Chandler turned back towards the office.

"Do you really want to go against your grandmother's wishes? She loved that Lodge and so did Hattie. And they both loved you."

The fight seemed to leave Chandler. Her shoulders sagged and she ran her hand through her hair. "I need air." She left the office and Lettie heard the front door slam.

Hillchamp watched her go and sighed, templing his fingers together on the desk. "I knew this would be a shock. You should know your own grandmother was in on this. It's why you didn't get it when she passed. They wanted you two to work together. You know friendship between your families goes back generations."

Oh, Lettie knew. "And died with mine, apparently."

Hillchamp chuckled. "The two of you were just girls the last time you saw each other. I think there's always room for a little grace when you meet someone again."

Was there? Or did bad blood stay in the system for life? "We can revisit it after the funeral. But I'm taking it."

"Good." He smiled. "I hate to see the way the town is going. What investors never realize until it's too late is that without the small-town charm the tourists leave, and we don't even have that many tourists to start with. There are a million other supe hot spots and most of them are a lot nicer than here. I suppose that's part of the problem though, land is still cheap in Lilac Lake."

That was true enough. "Do I need to sign anything?"

"If you don't mind."

When her grandmother had died, Lettie had been heartbroken that the Lodge wasn't mentioned in her will. She'd been mad at Hillchamp for being cagey. She'd called him every day for a week. She'd begged Everly to explain. And finally, she'd come to terms with the fact that the Stone and Sorcery was never going to be hers. Turns out Hattie had been conspiring all along.

When they were little girls Chandler and Lettie would play together at the Lodge, but even that had been filled with strife. Chandler was fearless and Lettie was not. Lettie didn't want to sneak out and climb the rocks, she didn't want to look for snakes at the shoreline. She wanted to play with dolls and swing on the tire hanging from the tree in the back.

And everything had gone downhill from there. They'd squabbled in middle school and by high school they weren't talking at all. Not until that one brief, shining moment at the end of Lettie's junior year and into summer. They hadn't meant to blow anything up.

Outside Hillchamp's office, the sun seemed brighter, the sky bluer, until Lettie turned a corner and Chandler was in her face.

"Did you know?" She'd zipped up her leather jacket over her white shirt. Closed off, just like she had always been. A universe unto herself.

Lettie was tired of it though. Eleven years had passed without a peep and now she thought she had the right to demand answers from Lettie? She pushed past Chandler. "Go talk to your snakes and stones and leave me alone."

"I tried," Chandler said, matching her pace as she turned onto Main Street.

"Oh, I know." Lettie didn't know why she was letting this get to her. She could honestly say she hadn't spent the last decade thinking about Chandler. She'd had her fair share of girlfriends since then and a whole, busy life. She stopped walking and put her hands on her hips. "If you sell the Lodge, I will never forgive you. *Never.* Be a silent partner. Go back to wherever the fuck you were. But I swear to God if you ever try to sell Stone and Sorcery, I will curse you."

Chandler blanched and Lettie thought maybe she had gone too far. She'd never actually curse her, maybe a hex, a small one. *Extremely small.* That might be worth pulling her magic out of retirement. Except she had no idea how to do a curse or a hex and doubted her mother or brother did either.

She toed a spot of grass, and the blade curled towards her. That part of her magic, her connection with nature, was the part she could never squash down. And that was okay with her, her connection to the earth had never scared her. Composing herself, she looked back up at Chandler. "Please. Don't."

"We'd have to work together." Chandler ran her hand through her dark curls again, making them frizz around her face.

"Could you even stand to stay in town?" She reached down, plucking one of the blades of grass, just for an excuse to take a step back.

"Listen, I get that this is bullshit, especially for you. I really do get that, Letts."

"Lettie."

Chandler sighed. "Fine. I really do get that, Lettie. And running the Lodge, silent partner or not, was certainly not in my five-year plan." Lettie scoffed at the idea of her having a five-year plan, but Chandler continued as though she hadn't noticed. Maybe she hadn't. "But can we meet there tomorrow? After the funeral?"

"Fine."

"And Lettie, please don't come."

Wow. Lettie opened her mouth. She closed it again. Then her grandmother's words rang through her head. *Don't judge the grieving, honey pie.* Sure, she'd spent more time with Everly than Chandler had, but she could mourn in her own way. And she'd been dreading going. Seeing one of her favorite people get put into the ground—she didn't want to do it again. "Fine. I'll meet you there at four."

"Fine."

-CHAPTER THREE-

"YOU CANNOT BE serious," Lettie's roommate and best friend, Daphne said. "You don't want to invest your life in building a business with that…*snake charmer.*"

"Please don't go into a rant on gorgons, Daph. *Please.*" Lettie loved Daphne, but the banshee's diatribes on gorgons often felt a lot closer to prejudice than any actual complaints. Lettie rarely bothered to argue though, she didn't think she'd be the one to end a two-hundred-year-old feud—especially when neither side seemed to remember what they were feuding over.

"I'm not. And it's not because she's a gorgon, it's because she's *her.*" Daphne curled her small body into the seat of her chair. "Seriously, Lettie."

But Lettie was *seriously* growing tired of talking about Chandler. She lit an incense stick and counted to ten, just to keep from talking, before she blew it out. "How did your date go?"

Magic sparkled around Daphne, silver and more pure than anything Lettie could hope to conjure. "Awful. Absolutely awful." The magic illuminated her white-blonde hair, making her look as otherworldly as the fae. "We won't be seeing each other again. I have nothing against humans but dating them can be so hard. Especially here, it's like they forget to leave tourist mode for the date. Maybe my sister is right, maybe I need to leave Lilac Lake."

"Shut your mouth!" Lettie chucked a pillow at her. "Anyway, how do I look?" She smoothed her dress. "Like a businesswoman?"

Daphne stood up and pulled her into a hug. "You look beautiful. And while I don't like her, you can run the Lodge. It's in your blood. You can do anything you put your mind to."

Lettie pushed her away. Daphne was always overly emotional, it was one of the things Lettie loved about her. You never had to wonder where you stood. "Stop. You're going to make me blush."

"Well, I better be the only one." Daphne released her. "You know, I saw Oak last night." Lettie stiffened at the mention of Chandler's once best friend. "They didn't even mention her being in town. I bet Chandler didn't tell them."

"Come on," Lettie begged. "Can we talk about something else? You know Lorne and Margery broke up again."

"No kidding. Is the Earth still revolving around the sun?" Daphne settled back in her seat. "Speak of the devil." She nodded towards the open window.

"How does he do that?" Sometimes it really seemed like Lettie could summon her brother just by thinking about him. Or maybe it was that he only lived three houses down and never had food in his fridge.

She opened the door before he could knock on it. Lorne was wearing a suit, the tie loosened around his neck. His sandy blonde hair was neater than usual, like he had styled it that morning, but several strands had fought their way free. "Where were you?" he asked, walking past her and winking at Daphne.

"Hey Lorne. She was here. Getting ready for her meeting with Chandler."

Lettie shot Daphne a look. "She asked me not to come to the funeral."

Lorne plopped down onto her couch and kicked off his shoes. "Damn, Lettie. She's been back two days and you're already letting her tell you what to do? I never did understand the hold that girl has on you. She's cute enough, but in a stabby, terrifying way."

"She doesn't have a hold on me." Lettie crossed her arms over her chest. "But it is her grandma and—"

"Bullshit!" Daphne said, her voice so shrill it made Lettie's ears ring. Banshee indeed. "Everly loved you just as much as her own grandchildren. I told you that you should have gone."

"Enough." Lettie had reached her breaking point. "Lorne Katz, you get your goddamn feet off my coffee table! And as for you—" She stuck her finger out and advanced on Daphne who didn't so much as blink. "You are supposed to be my best friend. And you're being an asshole."

"All I'm saying is—"

Lettie pressed her palms to her eye sockets and counted to five before removing them. "For the love of magic, I am not seventeen anymore. I do not jump when Chandler Hart says frog." Magic bounded through her veins—she couldn't get rid of it today—and her houseplants curled their vines towards her. "But I did not need to see Everly get lowered into the ground. I just saw my own grandma put in there six months ago. I know Everly loved me, and I loved her. And that's why I didn't need to go, because she's in my heart and she always will be."

"Well, damn," Lorne said, his feet still on her coffee table. "That is sweet. I just wanted to check in on you. You could have texted someone to say you weren't coming. Mama was all in state, buzzing around like a bee, probably half drunk, demanding to know what 'that Hart girl' had done with her baby."

"No," Daphne put her slim fingers in front of her mouth. "Please tell me Monica didn't make a scene at a funeral."

But Lettie didn't need to ask. Monica loved a scene. Being in one, watching one, causing one. Lettie loved her mother, but the woman was addicted to drama. She always had been. When Lettie was younger it had been embarrassing, but somewhere along the way she'd gotten used to it. Some people were just the way they were, and they were never going to change, and her mother was one of them.

Lettie's cuckoo clock chimed the hour, and dread tumbled down to her stomach. "Shit, I need to go soon."

"What are you going to say though?" Daphne asked.

And wasn't that the problem? Lettie didn't know. Lettie who always planned, who sent Daphne little color-coded bills for the rent every month, who had her books organized by both genre and alphabetical order, had no idea. And she had felt this way before. When her grandma had died and not left the Stone and Sorcery to her, Lettie had floundered. But then she'd planned again. She would buy her own shop, sell plants and trinkets and make a living.

Except she hadn't been able to afford much at all according to the bank, and everything she could afford ended up selling to someone with a better offer. And deep down, way, way down in the depths of her, she knew that wasn't what she wanted. She didn't want to sell plants; she wanted the Lodge. It was the only job she'd ever had, the only thing she'd ever really dreamed of. It was her home, even if she'd never actually lived there, she'd grown up there. Every inch of the Lodge held memories for Lettie.

Now she had no plan. She had rehearsed about a million conversations in her head the night before when she should have been sleeping, but none of them were right, none of them helped her sleep, because she couldn't begin to guess what Chandler would say.

"I'm just going to talk to her about the future," she said. "Lorne, don't eat all my food."

"Oh, you wound me." He grabbed the remote control. "Daph, mind if I stay?"

"Whatever." Daphne stood up and put her hands on Lettie's shoulders, grounding her. "Letts, remember, whatever happens today, whatever she says, The Lodge is yours. And the town is yours. We all believe in you."

"Okay." Lettie tried to make herself believe it. "Okay. Love you." She kissed Daphne's cheek and ruffled Lorne's hair.

"Wait!" Someone yelled, pulling Lettie out of her spiraling thoughts. She turned towards the sound to find Amelia running towards her.

Amelia owned The Three Sisters, the bar Lorne worked at. It was a town staple and the perfect job for her and the rest of her siren sisters.

During the off season she made money on booze and bar food, during spring and summer she rounded her sisters up, and they put on sequins and burlesque costumes, and sang their siren songs until everyone was turning their pockets out.

"Hey," Lettie said, glancing down the street.

"You okay?" Amelia asked, looking her over with pale gray eyes. "Your idiot brother told me what happened, and that's a lot, love. You know I adored your Grandma Hattie. No one could sing a show tune like her. And now Everly."

A lump rose in Lettie's throat. Was she okay? Mostly she was. She knew the two women were laughing together in the Beyond. But she missed them, their soft wrinkled hands, the way her grandma smelled of fresh packed earth and Everly smelled like brown sugar. "I'm getting by."

Without warning, Amelia pulled her into a hug, and it took all of Lettie's strength not to let herself melt into it. She wasn't sure if it was siren magic or just knowing that Daphne was right that kept her upright. But she had the people of Lilac Lake. People like Amelia who had known her for her entire life, and would always be there for her, no matter what happened with the Lodge.

"Of course you are. You're strong. But if you ever need a shoulder or an ear I'm here, and I have plenty of strong drinks." She released Lettie. "And speaking of drinks, for the next week you drink free at the Sisters."

"Thanks Amelia, seriously. I gotta go though." She managed to extract herself, but she wished she could follow Amelia back to the familiarity of the bar. She really could use a drink. Or a friend that wasn't Daphne, who knew her too well. Really, she just needed more time. If she had time to think she would have time to plan. And all she needed was a plan.

Instead Everly had died and thrown Lettie into the deep end. But, of course, she had. She could picture Everly and her grandmother hunched together, scheming and laughing and imagining how it would be when their granddaughters didn't have time to mourn because they'd be too mad.

"Dance when I'm gone, darling." Her grandma Hattie had told her near the end. *"Because I had it all."*

Lettie took a deep breath and yanked on her sleeves until they were properly in place. It was just Chandler, a woman she'd known her whole life. And the plan was to get her the fuck out of Lilac Lake as quickly as possible so Lettie could start her life.

Turning the corner, the chrome of Hershel's Diner came into view, blinding in the midday sun. She stopped before she made it to the door, Chandler was sitting by the window, absentmindedly tapping her finger against the ramekin of salt packets and turning it into stone and then back into ceramic. Again and again.

The truth was Chandler looked good. She'd always been beautiful, but age had thinned her face, and she carried herself with more confidence now—not that she'd been short on it in high school. Lettie wished she could say she didn't notice any of those things, but she did, because she'd always noticed Chandler, even when she didn't want to.

She steadied her nerves, and the magic rising within her. She wished she could squash it for good, but it was determined to make itself known, warming Lettie's stomach and making her feel light and airy.

The smell of syrup hit her as soon as she opened the door. She slid into the booth, her bare thighs catching on the aged vinyl. "Hey."

"Hey." Chandler frowned. "So…" She resumed her tapping, drumming her fingers against the table, and Lettie had to resist the urge to reach out and stop her.

Her long, strong fingers were another thing that Lettie remembered, the feeling of them the first time she had touched Lettie's face, how they had dug into her hips and pulled her close, lake water dripping from both of them, and Chandler had kissed her, and Lettie had felt like she was flying. And then Chandler had left, and for a while Lettie had felt like her wings had been clipped—before she'd realized she could fly just fine on her own.

Well, there was nothing to be done but jumping in feet first. "I've been thinking, and I figured you probably don't want to stay in Lilac Lake any longer than you—"

"Why?" Chandler's fingers stopped moving, and she leaned back in the booth. "Why do you figure I don't want to stay in Lilac Lake?" She raised that infernal eyebrow.

"Are you serious?" God, she was irritating. Lettie leaned back too, not breaking eye contact. "Because you took off as soon as you could. You've been gone for eleven years."

"Listen, Letts—"

"Lettie."

"Fine. Listen, *Leticia*, I know we've never been best friends, but I have just as much right to the Lodge as you do. And I don't plan on leaving you to do whatever you want with it."

"You're staying?" Lettie didn't mean for the words to come out as incredulously as they did. "I mean…" What did she mean? "I figured you had some grand life somewhere fabulous."

Chandler's face fell, her gaze dropping from Lettie's and onto the table. When the waitress came to take their order Lettie could have kissed her for providing a distraction. But then the waitress was gone, and they were alone again with only the clang of dishes and sizzle of bacon frying to fill the space between them. And that space seemed to grow by the second, so much bigger than just the cheap diner table and the plastic water cups. It was the space of two people who had wanted too much and never figured out how to have it, how to fit together without breaking pieces of themselves.

"I think the Lodge could really be something," Lettie said, hoping they could find common ground. "The cabins near the lake need work, but the bones are good. And there's already a staff. We didn't have to shut down when Everly died, so there's money coming in."

"Okay, yeah." Chandler pulled the container of sugar she had been fossilizing closer and pulled out a stevia pack, turning it between her fingers. Gold rings set with crystals covered her hands. Those hands irritated Lettie, drawing her eye, because this woman was infuriating, had always been infuriating.

Why did you leave? Lettie was surprised by how often the words kept forming on her tongue, begging for release. She thought she'd gotten over that particular sting a decade ago, but Chandler had always gotten under her skin, and the older they'd gotten the worse it had become. "How are we going to work together?" she whispered.

Chandler laughed. "We'll see what happens." There was something in her voice Lettie didn't like, it raised goosebumps on her arms and cooled the magic doing somersaults in her belly.

But she just smiled. She had six months to figure something out. Six months was plenty of time to get Chandler to leave the Lodge to her. All she had to do was play nice and stay calm. Which, admittedly, was not what she was historically good at, but there was a time for everything. "What do you say we get this lunch to go, and check out the property? I doubt you've been down to the docks in a while."

"I don't know." Chandler pulled her bottom lip between her teeth. "Yeah, fine. I guess that's the next logical step."

"Excellent." Lettie forced a smile onto her face. "I'll go let the waitress know."

-CHAPTER FOUR-

THE STONE AND Sorcery Lodge had been built by the hands of Chandler and Lettie's great grandfathers and renovated by their grandfathers. Both of them had heard the stories a million times, but for Lettie they had never grown old. The Lodge had always been special to her, a magical place where anything was possible. Nothing like the small, dilapidated cottage she shared with Daphne.

"I've always wanted to live on the property," Lettie said, following Chandler up the front steps.

She spun around so fast Lettie almost ran into her. Her green eyes were wide and as hard as stone, a sign Lettie had come to recognize as dangerous decades ago. "No."

"No?" Lettie pushed past her and up the stairs. "It's mine. I can live here." This was ridiculous. There were two owners' apartments off the lobby, and since both previous owners were dead, they weren't occupied.

"You have a house!" Chandler stood on the enormous wrap-around porch of the main building. "What about me?"

"Right." Lettie looked at her feet. The porch could use a fresh coat of paint. "Fine." She put her hands up. "I can wait six months if living in the same vicinity to me is that upsetting." She started to reach for the door and then stopped. Fuck that. "You know what, Chandler? You've got a lot of nerve! You fucking disappeared on me! That day was the scariest day of my life, and you were just gone. You wouldn't answer your phone, you wouldn't text me back. I never even saw you again, and now you act like you're owed the Lodge. I stayed! I took care of your grandma. I helped your mom when she moved! I was here, and you were…wherever the fuck you went. And now you come and act like I don't deserve to have this to myself."

"Lettie—"

"Oh? Do you have something to say now?"

Chandler took a step closer. Her mouth was a hard line. "Just that there are customers here. Not many, but…"

"Yeah. Cool. Fucking perfect really." Lettie turned and headed for the back of the porch. Bushes swayed as she passed. Her magic sparked, tiny bursts of pale green she hadn't seen in years. What was it about Chandler that made her want to scream, made her unable to control herself? How was this going to work? Everly and Hattie had been wrong, they couldn't work together.

In an attempt at self-control, Lettie breathed in the smell of the lake, algae and the lilac that bloomed near the cabins. She could not act like this. She was a grown woman. She could not strangle her business partner.

She went to the shore and stared out towards the island in the middle of Lilac Lake. How long had it been since she'd rowed over to it? Tourists loved it. The island was the source of their magic, the beating heart of Lilac Lake.

Every magic hub had one, but few were as literal as Lilac Lake's little island. And even fewer created the kind of creatures that her little town boasted of. Faeries and shifters sure, a dime a dozen. But banshees? Sirens? The only thing Lilac Lake had in common with places like Atlanta or New Orleans was witches.

Lettie pulled out her phone and opened her notes app. THINGS TO DO. She stared at the title and then her fingers flew across the screen. *Meet with an accountant and go over the books. Find a contractor to see if the cabins are structurally sound. Repaint the porch.*

"Hey."

Lettie kept typing. *Check the off-season reservations.*

"I should have said goodbye." Chandler's voice was low and mingled with the wind that blew across the lake. "You don't know what it's like, Lettie. You never did."

Gritting her teeth, she put her phone back in her pocket. She was going to have so much to tell Daphne. Preferably very drunk at The Three Sisters. Lettie kept her eyes on the island. "It doesn't matter. I got over it, Chandler. I spent most of my youth wishing you would love me, but I didn't waste my adulthood on it too. I don't need an explanation. But you aren't going to march back into town and tell me what I can and cannot do. Not here. Not in the place I've helped keep running."

"But that's what I'm saying, Lettie. I didn't talk to you, that doesn't mean I didn't talk to my grandmother. You don't get to decide what's best for both of us."

"I know you talked to her. I know every time you talked to her. But you made your choices, and they weren't here. You don't know this place anymore."

"There's a whole world out there." The wind blew Chandler's dark curls around her face. She was so sharp, she always had been, but without the baby fat on her face it was striking. "You should see it."

Lettie laughed, so piercing the leaves in the trees rattled with magic. "Jesus. Do you really think I'm such a small-town hick? I've traveled."

"You could travel more. We could fix this place up, sell it. We could make money, Lettie. There are investors—"

"Wow." Lettie shook her head. Her magic was no longer something friendly skittering along her skin, it boiled in her stomach. Or maybe that was rage. There were so many things she wanted to say—wanted to scream—but right now all she could see was a gorgon, hard and unfeeling. All the things they were rumored to be.

She turned from Chandler and headed back towards the Lodge, with its unruly ivy crawling up the walls and chipped paint, then paused at the entryway. Even though both of the old women she had loved were gone it still smelled like home, old wood, lilac and lavender. She could practically hear Hattie and Everly laughing. She sent a scowl towards the ceiling just for good measure. What had they been thinking?

But if she was completely honest, and not as pissed as she was at that moment, it was just like them, exactly the kind of thing they loved. There was a reason both of their daughters were prone to histrionics and shenanigans. They would have listened to Lettie bitch and moan, then they would have slapped her on the back and told her there was always a solution, always a way forward, if you just had grit and a good work ethic.

The hotel manager, Pepper, popped up from behind the front desk. Her dreads were twisted into a bun on top of her head, and it wobbled as she straightened. "Oh, well, welcome back. I heard the good news."

"That is yet to be seen." Lettie sighed. She had no right to pour all her troubles onto Pepper. She was fantastic, taking on more than her initial job description had required, and earning the promotions to prove it, even if Hattie and Everly had to make up position names to suit her.

Now, years later, Lettie didn't know what they'd do without her and her steady presence.

The front desk was smooth polished wood, and Lettie could still remember sitting there as a small child, kicking her feet back and forth above the floor, as she watched her grandmother work.

Her anger subsided, replaced with memories, nostalgia, and love. Chandler didn't have to understand the Lodge. Lettie did. "How's occupancy?" She asked, leaning over the desk to grab a folder labeled "TO DO." Lettie loved a To-do list.

"Low, but it always is this time of year," Pepper said, clicking on something Lettie couldn't see on her computer. "Tourist season is already half booked. Everly had been thinking about running a special before…" Pepper frowned. "Well, I figured I'd hold off until I spoke to you. As much as I loved the old H and E, this place could use a few upgrades, and I figured it would be best to have fewer guests while we do them."

"That's why we pay you the big money." Lettie grinned and Pepper pulled a face. "Well, the medium money. Yeah, I've got a few things I need to take care of—"

One of those things blew in, her steps rattling as if her shoes were full of pebbles. "Pepper." Chandler nodded towards the front desk. Her jaw was tight, her eyes stone, and she didn't so much as glance at Lettie. "I'd like to stay in one of the apartments. Can I get the key?"

Pepper glanced between Lettie and Chandler; her brown eyes wide. Lettie nodded. "And I'll take my Gran's." Unlike Chandler, Lettie knew exactly where the keys were, and she snatched one off the wall and headed into the kitchen. It was empty but smelled like cinnamon and yeast. She pushed open the door to the narrow hallway that led to the owners' suites and marched right to her grandmother's old home.

And paused.

What was she doing? Was she going to live here just to spite Chandler? Daphne would murder her if she left her behind. If anyone should stay at the Lodge, it was Lorne. God only knew how he paid his rent. But that was something for another moment, and at this moment the apartment felt like something she'd earned.

Inside the apartment smelled just like Hattie. So much so that Lettie had to steady herself on an old chair to keep her knees from buckling. She missed her grandmother. And Hattie would have never let her home look like this. Though half the furniture had been moved out, what remained was covered in a thin layer of dust.

She found cleaner under the sink, pulled on her grandmother's old gloves and got to work scrubbing, wiping, and trying her best not to cry or think of Chandler. This was a task she could complete. Even if she didn't live at the Lodge, she would be spending more time there. Having her own space would be nice.

An hour into cleaning someone knocked on the door, and Lettie froze. "Lettie, you better not be doing anything weird because I'm coming in," Lorne said, his voice muffled.

"What would she even be doing?" Daphne hissed.

Lettie pulled the door open and looked over the two of them. "Why are you here?" Behind them she could see the door to Everly's old apartment. Chandler hadn't pulled it closed and she could hear music she didn't recognize coming through.

"Getting you out of your head," Daphne said, pushing past Lettie and into the apartment.

"I don't know much, but I know when you're about to have a breakdown. And don't argue," Lorne said, pulling the door shut behind him. "Because if you do, I'm gonna call Mama."

"You are not."

"No, I'm not. Because we're going to the Three Sisters, and you're going to have a drink or two, and you're going to—" He froze, looking around the apartment. With a gulp, he picked up a little figurine of a cat, one of Hattie's trinkets, and turned it over in his hands, then sat it down and ran his fingers through his hair. "Shit, Letts, you shouldn't have done this on your own."

Lettie and Lorne's mother, Monica, had always been a bit of a mess but it had only gotten worse when their father had passed away. She was a decent mother, always there, just not very good at the things mothers were supposed to be good at, so Hattie had stepped in, making sure both of them were taken care of.

"I don't want to talk about it." Lettie grabbed the bucket she had been using and headed for the sink. "And I don't want to go to The Three Sisters."

"Too bad." Daphne took the bucket and dumped the water down the drain. "She doesn't get to fly into town and turn everything upside down."

Lettie was getting a headache. "I'm busy and I'm not discussing this, which is why I didn't call either of you. You're just a bunch of busybodies who need more regular employment."

"I'm going to count to three," Lorne said, and Daphne laughed.

"No, you aren't, you oversized baby." Lettie took off her gloves and laid them on the sink to dry. "Maybe I'll call Mama and tell her what a pest you're being. Tell her that you aren't seeing Margery anymore and that maybe she can set you up with—"

"Who said I wasn't seeing Margery?"

"Margery did."

"Well, shit."

"Who gives a fuck?" Daphne moved in between the two of them. Lorne opened his mouth to speak, but she snapped her fingers. "Lettie, you are going to go to The Three Sisters. Ach! Don't talk. I don't care.

We're going. We're going to drink tequila and make a list of everything you need to do and that's that. I'm invoking best friend privileges."

"*Don't.*" But part of Lettie did want to go to The Three Sisters. Daphne was right. She was getting all twisted up. Every problem had a solution. And while it wasn't likely she was going to find it at the bottom of a bottle of tequila, she had to start somewhere. "Okay, fine."

"Yay!" Daphne clapped her hands.

-CHAPTER FIVE-

DESPITE DAPHNE'S BEST efforts to stretch out the getting ready stage of the evening, it was still fairly early when they got to the bar. Amelia was behind the counter, a rag slung over her shoulder.

"Good grief, Lorne. Even on your day off?"

"Fuck you, Amelia. I'm supporting my sister." But there was no bite to his voice. Though Lorne had a group of friends he hung out with occasionally, usually to the detriment of all the furniture in his apartment, Lettie suspected Amelia was his best friend.

The smile on Amelia's face said Lorne might be hers as well. Though the bar was called The Three Sisters, it was Amelia's; her sisters Aria and Alice only showed up for performances and occasionally drinking. The running of the bar was all Amelia.

"Finally going to let a banshee join you up on stage?" Daphne asked, sliding into one of the barstools.

"Yeah, girl. I'm always looking for ways to lose money." Amelia brushed a strand of her dark red hair out of her face. "Is it a wine night or a tequila night? Or midafternoon as the case may be?"

"We had to get good seats to see the best siren performance this side of the Mississippi." Daphne winked. "And tequila."

Lettie wasn't sure if she was in the mood to watch Daphne flirt with both her brother and Amelia all night long, but she didn't think she was going to get much of an option either way. Plus watching Daphne flirt was just part of being around Daphne.

Ugh. Lettie silently chastised herself for being so disagreeable. What was her problem anyway? This was not the Lettie she wanted to be, angry and bitter. She slid into the seat beside Daphne. Her life was not so bad. She was young. She was fun. She reached up, pulled the ponytail holder from her hair, and shook out her strawberry blonde hair. "Amelia, is Aria coming by tonight."

Daphne swiveled in her chair, wiggling her eyebrows suggestively while Amelia leaned on one elbow. "Yeah, I think she's coming by with Margery. Why, Lettie Katz, do you ask?"

"Yes, indeed. Why?" Daphne was grinning like a cat who caught a canary.

Because of several reasons, all of which Lettie was not about to tell Aria's sister. All three sisters were older than Lettie, and Aria was the oldest. When Lettie was twelve Aria had spent the summer as the lifeguard at the lake, so Lettie had spent the entire summer on the shore and only pretended to drown once.

And now Chandler was back with her long fingers and her dark hair and her maddening personality, and Lettie needed something, anything, to get Chandler off her mind.

She shrugged. "Haven't seen her in a while. I heard she was doing accounting for Hershel."

"Yep." Amelia turned, grabbing a bottle, and poured them both shots. "Neither of you is driving, correct?"

"Amelia, I live three blocks away. Be serious." Lettie took the shot and downed it, letting the burning of the alcohol combine with the burning magic in her belly. Stupid magic. Stupid bad timing magic. What did it want with her, anyway?

"So, I heard you're finally—*officially*—taking over the Lodge." Amelia grabbed the ingredients for what she called a 'low-class margarita' and started mixing.

"Hopefully, I don't destroy the Katz legacy."

Lorne slapped her on the back. "Don't worry. Mama already did that."

"On the house. For a new business owner." Amelia winked and slid the murky green drink across the bar. "Your Grandma and Everly were never into it, but I think we could do some amazing events. You've got all that space out by the lake, and I've got the booze and the talent connections."

"I've been saying that! We should have, like, a real event! Not just some weird tourist trap but a 'Palooza or something," Daphne said, leaning her elbow on the bar.

Lilac Lake had its faults—mainly its lack of non-fried foods or clothing stores with things Lettie would actually wear, but sometimes, in moments like these, there was more magic than just what emanated from the lake. There was a legacy, deep roots that couldn't be shaken. Watching her friends make jokes with each other, and the shared sense of belonging that came from growing up together.

Lettie wasn't sure when she'd become a recluse, but it had been sometime after her Gran had died. She'd been so determined to find a back-up plan when she didn't think she was getting the Stone and Sorcery that she'd let the rest of her life fall away. The only reason she hadn't truly faded into the background was Daphne.

Being small and quiet was nearly impossible when your best friend was a banshee, especially if that banshee happened to be Daphne Dixon, former prom queen and current complete mess. And Lettie loved her for her. Her whole life Daphne had evened her out, kept her from forgetting that fun was important too.

So, she let herself have fun.

So much fun that by the time Margery and Aria showed up she was five drinks deep and shoving quarters in the jukebox with Daphne. Aria looked beautiful, with the same red hair as her sister, big brown eyes, and a dress that Lettie would never be able to pull off.

And like always, Lettie had taken one look at her, blushed so hard she could feel the heat in her face, and scooted closer to Daphne out of pure terror. Except tonight the terror hadn't come, just thoughts of another woman with stupid snake tattoos and an attitude so bad Lettie wanted to shake her.

"Well, at least Lorne's getting laid tonight," Daphne tried to whisper in Lettie's ear, failing spectacularly, but the voices of the growing crowd drowned her out. "You should talk to her," Daphne said, inclining her head at Aria.

"No way," Lettie said, reaching down and gripping Daphne's wrist. Okay, maybe Aria still evoked a certain degree of terror in her. "I think she has a boyfriend."

"Psh," Daphne said, but she wrapped her arm around Lettie's shoulder and led her in the other direction. "We should go swimming. It's a full moon. The perfect night."

"It's fifty degrees out." Lettie reminded her, but she could see the mischief in Daphne's eyes. "Why don't we—"

"Shit! Shit!" Daphne tried to push Lettie behind her, so violently and suddenly that bright green magic sparked at Lettie's fingertips. She dug her fingers into Daphne's shoulders, trying to peer over her. "She's here!" The words were a banshee screech that left several people nearby wincing.

Lettie scanned the crowd, unsure of what she should expect. Everly's ghost? Her mother? The latter chilled her to her bones. But it was Chandler she found. She had on tight black jeans and a slinky silk top. Her curls looked freshly washed, less frizzy than they had been. Maybe she'd stopped running her hands through them.

And beside her was Oak. They'd been Chandler's best friend in high school, and she knew they had kept up with her, but she didn't realize the two of them were close enough to come out for drinks.

When Oak spotted Lettie their face moved strangely, from the smile they usually wore, to something closer to a grimace as they glanced at Chandler. Their honey curls were cut short, though the buzz on the sides had grown out. They shoved their hands into their jeans and gave Lettie a shrug.

So much for fading into the crowd. Chandler was staring right at her. "Did you have to scream?" she tried to whisper to Daphne, but she was drunk.

"Fuck this." Daphne shrugged out of Lettie's grasp and made her way through the crowd, her white-blonde hair swaying.

After a lifetime of friendship with Daphne, Lettie still found it hard to guess what was going to come out of her mouth, but she knew whatever it was wasn't going to be good. She tried to reclaim her grasp on Daphne, but she slipped through the crowd more easily than Lettie and got to Chandler first.

"What even is your problem?" Daphne wasn't as tall as Chandler, but she still managed to sneer at her.

"Wha—Daphne?" Chandler blinked.

"Daphne, I don't think—" Oak began, a blush creeping over their brown cheeks, but Daphne glared at them, and they clamped their lips shut.

"You've always thought you were so much better than everyone. And for what?" Daphne stuck one hand on her hip.

Time seemed to move slowly, or maybe it was Lettie's limbs, but eventually she managed to make her way across the bar. "Daphne. *Stop it.*" This wasn't what she wanted at all.

The bar had grown quiet, only the music played, a horrible old doo-wop number Daphne had queued up on the jukebox that didn't match the mood at all. She definitely wouldn't be hitting on Aria tonight because the siren was looking at her through the crowd and she didn't look amused. Embarrassment settled in Lettie's stomach.

"Fine. But I'm watching you." Daphne pointed her fingers at her eyes and then at Chandler, and Lettie wanted to sink into the floor.

"Can I…speak to you." Chandler hitched her thumbs into the pockets of her jeans.

There were two options. Just fucking run away and hope she had managed to get to black out levels of drunk or talk to Chandler alone in a bar—also drunk. Lettie didn't like either option.

"I think the show is about to start," Lettie slurred, which made no sense, yet the words tumbled ineloquently out of her mouth.

Chandler narrowed her eyes, and Oak tapped their foot on the sticky wooden floor. "Lettie…"

"Fine." She threw her hands up, too wide, too erratically, and headed for the front door.

Outside the air was cool, but still muggy, a reminder that summer was always right around the corner in the south. She leaned her head against the brick exterior of The Three Sisters. "I can't control Daphne."

"Sure." Chandler's jaw was set and there was a hiss to her voice. Was it hard to be a gorgon out in the world? There were so few. Did she tell people? Did they notice or just assume she was a witch? "We need to stop fighting, Lettie."

"Promise you'll sell the Lodge to me." She tried to look intimidating but wasn't sure she pulled it off.

Chandler sighed, casting her eyes towards the stars. "Listen, I'm here for a while. Not that it's your business, but things are…I'm staying in Lilac Lake for a while. Why don't we revisit this in a few months? See where we're at."

Lettie scoffed, and magic sparked. Good goddess, what the hell was going on with her? But Chandler jumped back, and Lettie couldn't help but laugh. "You fucking left, and I had to watch them rebuild the goddamn town square, you know? You should have seen the way everyone looked at me. Believe me, I was not the golden girl then."

Chandler's mouth twitched and her eyes softened. "It wasn't your fault. How were we supposed to know the gazebo would blow up?"

"I think it *was* our fault, Chandler. Like…it was absolutely our fault. In fact, you can ask my mom because she still talks about the bill they sent her."

"Well, that's one thing we have in common. I still hear about that one too."

Lettie laughed, but then silence fell between them again. And what was there to say? They had been kids then. A decade had passed since they had last spoken. Now they had this big, huge, thing they were supposed to undertake together, but how did you do that with someone you had never found your footing with?

"I thought about you," Chandler said, her voice low and nearby the blades of grass rattled. Lettie didn't know if it was her magic or Chandler's that caused it.

"I don't want to hear that. I really don't. It was just weird seeing you, but I'm not that teenager that follows you around anymore." She squeezed her eyes shut for a moment, trying to make her foggy brain focus on what actually needed to be done. "But we can't put this off for months. We need to work in the off season. Why don't I come over to the Lodge tomorrow and we'll talk about my ideas for updates?"

"Our ideas."

Lettie shrugged, and this time she knew it was her magic that made the last of the leaves rustle overhead. "I'm the one who's staying. Noon?"

"Fine."

She pushed herself off the wall, and found her legs wobbly but working, and went back inside. The sisters were on the stage, their voices better than any drug, and Lettie let it wash over her.

She danced to the siren's song, gripping Daphne for support. But between songs her thoughts crept back in. If she could choose, things would be better between her and Chandler. She'd co-own the Lodge with someone who loved it as much as her.

But she couldn't change it, not if Chandler didn't want things to be amicable between them. She left the dance floor and Daphne and Lorne followed, sliding into chairs on either side of her.

Lettie let her eyes drag across the three redheads as they moved like liquid across the stage. She'd never had grace like that. And what she had said to Daphne was true, she was tired of talking about Chandler, of even thinking about her. The gorgon seemed to have consumed her brain. She took another shot of tequila. She'd think about everything tomorrow when the sun burned her retinas and her head pounded.

But not tonight.

-CHAPTER SIX-

EVEN ON DAYS with minimal guests, the Stone and Serpent Lodge had breakfast in the dining room, and that was all that was keeping Lettie going. After her little run-in with Chandler, she'd kept drinking until way too late into the night.

She remembered dancing, the siren sisters twisting and laughing in the crowd. She remembered Lorne with Margery in his lap. She barely remembered coming home, but she remembered how good the bed had felt when she'd curled into it.

Daphne was still passed out across her grandmother's floral couch, making Lettie glad that banshee snores didn't work like banshee screams.

She contemplated waking Daphne up, but she was fairly sure the reason she'd insisted on sleeping at the Lodge was to yell at Chandler some more, and Lettie simply wasn't in the mood. She could handle all her yelling on her own.

Wrapping her arms around herself, she took in her surroundings. The Lodge apartment was much nicer than the tiny place they shared. And did Lorne really need it? He'd just make it as gross as his own apartment, and it did him some good to have bills to pay. If anyone needed to learn responsibility, it was her brother. And it would be so much easier to run the Lodge if she lived on site.

She filed the thought in her mind, deciding to ask Daphne about it once her head wasn't pounding and the light of the sun didn't seem like a personal assault.

Lettie pulled her grandmother's robe out of the closet and held it in her hands. She had never seen her grandmother wear it, but still it hung in her closet and smelled of her. It would be strange to wear it, however, the alternative was walking out into her own establishment in the clothes she'd worn the night before. And they reeked in all the ways bar clothes reeked the next morning.

If she was going to keep staying here, she needed to move some more stuff over. Lettie clutched the robe tighter. *Hers.* A legacy. Something real and tangible.

She tightened the belt of the robe. It was beautiful, embroidered silk and soft as butter. Lettie pushed open the door to the hallway and came face to face with Oak.

"Oh." They clutched a croissant to their chest. "Listen, Lettie I—Shit, I don't know. I just hope we're good."

"Yeah, of course." Lettie and Oak had never been close, but they'd known each other since they were kids. They had lived two houses down and were one of the few shifters in Lilac Lake. Lettie had no problem with Oak, and unlike Daphne, she wasn't going to manufacture one.

There were so many questions rolling around in her head and unfortunately the most indiscreet one slipped out. "You spent the night?"

"Not like that," Oak said, still clutching the croissant. They tightened their grip and little flakes of crust fell to the ground. "I mean, we're just friends. I think I'm gonna go in. But, uh…"

"We're good," Lettie said, hoping to put them out of their misery, and they slipped back inside the apartment.

Well, that was incredibly weird and awkward. Living across from Chandler was not going to be ideal. But again, thoughts for when she was less hungover. Lettie headed towards the aroma of coffee, making little lists in her head: places the floor needed to be buffed, furniture they could get rid of to open up the space, colors to paint the walls. Making lists made her head feel better.

The dining room was mostly empty except for an older woman perusing the platter of muffins. Lettie smiled, imagining the space filled with guests, children dripping from the lake, couples making their way to the swings she would install on the porch. Spring and summer were always busy, but she enjoyed it. As long as the guests were happy, they were usually kind, and she intended to keep them happy.

"What do you think?" the woman asked, "Banana nut or blueberry?"

"I'm a banana nut girl. Always have been," Lettie said, grabbing a ceramic mug and pouring herself a cup of coffee.

"Interesting little town. I still remember when the owners of this place exposed all the…the others. I always said I'd come visit. I wanted to meet such interesting women. I'm sorry I missed them."

"Me too." Lettie stirred in sugar. "I'm Lettie Katz. My grandmother owned this place."

"Oh, what a fun life you must have had. Well, this is a beautiful inn. You have a good day, sweetheart. I think someone is waiting to talk to you." She gestured over Lettie's shoulder and grabbed a banana nut muffin.

Lettie turned, expecting Pepper, but it was Chandler, leaning against the doorframe, no makeup, her hair shoved into a messy bun, watching Lettie. "Oh."

"You're good with them. My grandma always said you were. Said I should watch you, learn how to talk to people."

"Everly was a smart woman."

"I never wanted you to hate me, Lettie. I still don't want that." Chandler stood straighter. "I never thought they would leave the Lodge to me."

Lettie scoffed. "Come on, of course you did. They told us from the cradle." She wrapped her hands around the steaming mug of coffee.

"Would you be able to buy me out?"

For a fair price? Lettie didn't think so. She had a modest down payment she had planned to use for whatever business she bought, but she'd need it for upgrades. And all of those businesses were much smaller than Stone and Sorcery, certainly much smaller than what half of it would cost. "Listen, I'm sick of talking about this. I just need some time to think."

"Fair enough." Chandler poured her own cup of coffee. "First thing is we need to import some beans. This isn't it."

"Oh yeah. Nothing old southerners love better than imported beans." She glanced up at Chandler, who had gone still, the carafe of creamer in her hand. "I'm kidding. You can make the coffee choices."

Maybe there was a little spot she could pry into, some middle ground where they could coexist without arguing. Lettie was almost thirty years old, she'd been seventeen the one and only time she'd slept with Chandler. She could do this. And maybe Chandler would stay. Maybe there would be no selling of the Lodge. It wasn't ideal; she wanted it to herself, to hoard it like a dragon, but the Lodge was meant to be run by a Katz and a Hart. It always had been.

And maybe Chandler was thinking the same thing because she nodded. "Cool. Do you still make those lists?"

"Yeah." Lettie nodded. "Of course. And I've been working on a to-do list, if you're interested?" Chandler nodded and Lettie continued. "I know there are funds for upgrades, though I haven't gone over the books to get any exact numbers. I think if we get the cabins in working order by summer, we should be able to finance all the renovations the Lodge needs. It won't be enough to do a complete renovation, but we can afford an extensive update, get some new appliances for the kitchen, have someone look at the plumbing, update the furniture."

"I'm so glad you said that." Chandler tucked a stray strand of hair behind her ear. "Because look, I love vintage, but some of these couches are…"

"Past their prime," Lettie offered while Chandler searched for words. "Listen, I know you didn't like the idea, but I think I'm going to move in here too. My apartment…well, it sucks, and it's like feet away from Lorne's house, and he eats all my food."

"Will Daphne be moving in too?" Chandler frowned. "You know she hates me. She's always hated me." A crease had formed between Chandler's eyebrows, growing deeper with each word.

It was true that Daphne hated Chandler, though Lettie couldn't see any sense in confirming her suspicions. "I mean…we've always been roommates. And there's three bedrooms."

"Really? Always? Come on." Chandler headed towards the entrance and Lettie followed.

"Yeah, seriously. I didn't go to college, and I had to get out of my mom's house, so first it was me and Lorne and Daphne—" Lettie smiled, remembering those days full of ramen noodles and sleeping on air mattresses. They'd been drunk on freedom—and cheap beer. The entire world had seemed spread before them, just waiting for them to figure out how to take it.

"Jesus." Chandler pulled the front door open. The air was crisp, the humidity finally giving way to a winter chill. Though Lettie didn't mind the heat too much, the few months of cold were always a welcome relief to the sweltering summer sun and the relentless busyness of tourist season.

"Yeah. But Lorne is a terrible roommate, even worse when my mom isn't around to clean up after him, so we suggested he might have more fun living with his friends. Then it was just me and Daphne." Lettie pushed herself onto the porch railing and her toes grazed the wood planking below.

"Do you…never mind."

"What?" This was the best conversation they'd had since Chandler had come back. Lettie didn't want it to end. She liked the pleasant moments with Chandler, she always had. Unfortunately, the bad ones were never far behind when it came to the two of them, like no matter how hard they tried they could never get in sync.

"I don't think it's really my business." Chandler leaned against the wall across from Lettie. She looked just as carefree as she had in high school. Lettie had always admired the ease Chandler carried herself with, she could never hope to achieve it. Lettie was and always had been, a ball of nerves. She wasn't sure if it was clinical or just a symptom of being raised by a mother who never worried about anything at all. Probably both.

But her curiosity was piqued. "Now I have to know." Lettie sipped her coffee, and she knew she was staring, but how could she stop when she knew this moment would break? There'd be something else to argue over, or someone would walk through the door, and they'd be back at each other's throats.

Whatever came next, this was worth savoring, a chilly morning, a hot cup of coffee, a conversation with a beautiful woman about their business. This was a life she wanted to lead, even if her business partner was extremely prickly around the edges.

"Well…" Chandler cleared her throat. "Are you in love with her? In high school it seemed like—"

"Daphne?" Lettie couldn't stop the laugh that escaped her throat. "Oh, no. No. Not at all. She's…Well, she doesn't date, not that I want to date her. But no, she's just my best friend."

"Oh, okay." Chandler shrugged.

Awkward silence stretched between them, filled with early morning birdsong. Underneath the porch the grass rustled, the old familiar refrain of being near Chandler. Snakes followed wherever she went. Or maybe it was Lettie's magic, the earth stretching towards her. It was growing harder to tell.

"You said you lived in the city. Are the snakes there? Do people know?" Lettie regretted the words as something flashed in Chandler's eyes. She had no idea what Chandler's life had been like outside of Lilac Lake and asking if she was an outcast probably wasn't the best way to broach the subject.

Chandler cleared her throat and adjusted her septum ring. "Not many. I don't tell them, but they figure it out sometimes. And it's not—it's nice to be back. It's different here."

Stay. The word came easily to Lettie, but voicing it was so much harder. And she didn't know if she meant it, or if she was just afraid of running the Lodge all by herself. So, she asked another question. "Why'd you come back?"

"Same reason anyone does anything. A girl broke my heart." Without a word, Chandler walked off the porch and towards the lake.

Lettie hesitated. Did she need space? But the worst that could happen was Chandler would yell at her and that was nothing new, so she jumped down and followed. "I bet it was a human. All my worst heartaches were from humans."

Chandler stopped and turned towards Lettie. For a second, she was sure she was right—Chandler was going to yell at her. Instead, she laughed. "Yeah. She was. I'm not sure if it was the snakes, or turning things to stone, or just the general fucked-upness of my life but she'd had enough of me. Said I was a frightening mess."

"Well, she's not wrong." Lettie brushed her fingers against a rosebud as they walked by it, tickling the petals.

"Well fuck you, Katz. And I believe it was your magic that did most of the explosion."

"Me? The whole thing turned to stone, Chandler! That one cop said it looked like we blew up a quarry."

"Well, you'll be happy to know I haven't accidentally turned anything to stone since—" Chandler swallowed, a lump in her throat bobbing. "Since I left Lilac Lake." She quickened her pace.

That was the truth between them, the thing that neither could deny. No matter how hard they tried to get along they were volatile together, explosive and dangerous.

"Where are you going?" Lettie asked. Chandler was taller than her and Lettie was practically jogging to keep up.

And the other part, the thing that nagged Lettie each time she tried to let her guard down—could she trust Chandler? Had the gorgon really changed since they were teenagers, or would she still run off at the first sign of trouble? When the going got tough would Chandler stick around, or leave Lettie, once again, cleaning up the pieces of a mess they both made?

"I don't know." Chandler stopped walking. But Lettie kept moving. She crashed into Chandler, and she grabbed Lettie steadying her with a hand on her arm. Chandler dropped her grip slowly, brushing her fingers against the silk of the robe. Those infernal fingers. "Where did you get this thing?"

"It was my Gran's. None of my clothes are here." Lettie looked up. She'd forgotten how green Chandler's eyes were. *Shit*. She stepped away from the gorgon. "I should go. Back up—back to the house."

"Lettie—" She pulled her bottom lip between her teeth. "Yeah, you should go. But… dinner later."

Dinner? With Chandler? "Yeah, we can talk about the cabins like we meant to."

"Okay. Yeah, that sounds good."

Lettie turned before Chandler finished talking and clutched her coffee cup until she was worried it would shatter. The ever-blooming lilac swayed as she walked past, the petals shaking, as though even the plants could sense the way her stomach was clenching.

Because Lettie felt seventeen again. Catching up to a girl she'd spent years chasing. She'd never had anything good with Chandler—whether rivals or hesitant lovers, they were explosive, too different, too…too much for each other.

A decade without thinking about her had made it easy to forget. But how were they going to run to Lodge? Lettie needed money, whether she had to beg, borrow or steal. She needed to find a way to buy Chandler out. She could not blow up the Lodge the way the two of them had blown up town square.

She squashed her magic down as it rumbled in her belly. It had never given her anything but pain and now it bubbled again, wishing to find a way out. But she wasn't a teenager, she was a grown woman, and this time she would be in control. This time her magic didn't stand a chance.

She kept her head down, as she rushed into the Lodge, not making eye contact with anyone. She kept her hands balled in fists at her side as she headed straight towards her apartment and the safety and comfort it offered.

-CHAPTER SEVEN-

THE DOOR SLAMMED behind Lettie, waking Daphne. She stretched her arms above her head, then rubbed her eyes. "This place is so much nicer than our apartment. It smells like coffee in the morning, not old farts."

"Daph—" But Lettie didn't know what she wanted to say. She wasn't even sure what she was thinking. She had just known she had to get away from Chandler and catch her breath.

"What's wrong?"

"I don't think I can do this." She fell into a wingback chair and sighed. "Why would Gran spring this on me?"

"One last prank." Daphne pulled her feet under her. "We could kill Chandler. Just—" She dragged her fingers across her neck. "Take her out. I'll be your partner."

"Maybe you could buy her out," Lettie said, hope rising and then falling just as quickly. Daphne worked part time at the library and made up the rest waitressing. She couldn't afford the Lodge.

"Honey. Darling. I love you so much." Daphne smiled, a bit too wide to be human. "But part of your problem is you've never had a real job."

"Yes, I have. I work here."

"On salary. For your grandmother. Like I said, I love you, but this is a lot of responsibility to just drop in your lap and it dropped along with your ex. You know you're allowed to panic a little bit, right? You don't always have to know what to do."

But someone *did* have to know what to do, and that someone had always been Lettie. She'd prided herself on it. But going into business with Chandler felt like jumping off a cliff without knowing what was at the bottom. "I'm not just being nervous about the Lodge, Daph. She's always had something over me and I've never wanted her to. She doesn't even like me, and I don't like her but—" She pushed herself out of the chair and headed for the window.

Daphne crept up behind Lettie on silent feet. "Normally I'd advise you to just fuck her and get it out of your system, but I do appreciate this is a more delicate situation." She rested her head on Lettie's shoulder and the familiar scent of Daphne filled her nose, rose-scented perfume and a hint of cinnamon.

"Look at you, growing." Lettie sighed, but her exhaustion wasn't physical, it was mental. Her problems were so much bigger than a conversation with Daphne could fix. "We should move in here."

"Oh, thank God." Daphne threw her arms around Lettie, hugging her from behind. "I was so scared you were going to leave me behind and I love it here. I love it so much. You can see the lake. Plus, there's an extra bedroom, and a full kitchen." She kissed the top of Lettie's head.

"And no rent," Lettie said. "So, you could finish your degree. No more waiting tables." She tried to squirm out of Daphne's grip, but the banshee held firm. "But you know she'll be our neighbor, right?"

"For six months. Whatever. But who is going to tell Lorne?"

"Poor Lorne." He was going to have to walk twice as far to steal their food.

"Leticia Katz!"

They both froze at the sound on the other side of the door, and Daphne pantomimed climbing through the window.

"I could scream," Daphne whispered, her face in an exaggerated grimace. "I know it's illegal, but desperate times call for desperate measures."

"We could swim to the island. Live there, right on top of the magic. It might be nice."

The door handle shook. "Lettie! You let me in right this moment."

There was nowhere to go for either of them, though Daphne's eyes were darting around the room, searching for an escape. There was only the door between them. Between Lettie and the thing she dreaded the most. The person she had been avoiding since she'd sat in Hillchamp's office and had her life turned upside down.

Her mother.

But there was no other choice. Lettie knew she could either open the door or a Monica Katz sized hole would soon appear in it. She gripped the handle while Daphne scurried deeper into the apartment.

Honestly, her mother wasn't that bad, she was just a lot. A whole lot. More than Lettie wanted to deal with at the moment, when everything already felt so heavy, because her mother made everything *a situation.*

She jerked the door open, and her mother pulled her into a floral scented embrace before quickly releasing her.

"My darling daughter." Monica didn't wait for an invitation before barging in. "What are you doing at your grandma's house? Lorne said this was where I should look for you, but I almost didn't believe him."

Lettie realized she was still wearing Everly's robe and shrugged it off. "They left me the Lodge." Her magic flickered at her fingertips, and she balled her fists to keep her mother from seeing it. The insistent barrage of magic was something she could put on a back burner—unless Monica saw it.

"What?" Monica crossed her arms. And then her face lit into a smile. "Oh, well, that's wonderful, my sweet baby. You let me know if you need anything. Are you staying here? Of course you are! This is better than that old apartment of yours and—"

"Mom…mom!" Lettie took a deep breath. "I just found out. Chandler and—"

"Chandler? What is she doing here? Ginger didn't mention that to me at all. I can't believe all of you are keeping this from me! Where is she?" She looked around as though expecting to see Chandler hiding underneath the coffee table.

"She's in Everly's apartment."

"Well, the two of you are going to be neighbors, are you? Ginger will be so pleased, you know. Does she know? Please, don't tell me that you haven't told Ginger either, because—"

"Mom!" Maybe Lettie *should* leave Lilac Lake. The thought often came to her when she was trying to rise above the swelling tide of her mother's ego. "I have no idea what she told Ginger."

"Well, I know I like to razz you about the town square, and I know the two of you like to argue, ever since you were little girls—I never could understand it, generations of women getting along, but the two of you were oil and water." She clapped her hands together. "Anyway, the point is you can do this." She stepped closer. Lettie felt a swooping in her stomach that had nothing to do with magic.

"What are you doing?" She could see magic on her mother's fingers.

Monica took Lettie's face in her hands and planted a kiss on her forehead. "You are both motivated, bright women. This town needs a renovation—the proper kind, the kind with heart, not the kind out-of-town assholes bring, and you can do it. You can do so much."

Pride swelled in Lettie, against her will. Her mother had a lot of flaws, but Lettie's love of Lilac Lake and her belief in the power of community came from her mother. "I know I can run the Lodge. I know that, but…"

Monica's hands fell to Lettie's shoulders. "Your heart is not as fragile as you think it is, and your magic has never been a curse. Whatever happens the world will turn, the sun will rise, and you will be okay."

"Not if I explode." God, she didn't want to discuss this with her mother, but maybe she had a point. Maybe that was why she'd been avoiding her since she found out she had inherited the Lodge. Monica believed in facing things head on, and she knew plenty about heartbreak. Lettie had been too young to remember when her father died, but she knew it had almost broken her mother. Yet Monica had kept going, she'd thrived.

"You were both children then. Are you scared you'll do something to the Lodge? The Lodge has stood through Hattie and Everly. The two of you won't destroy it." She gave Lettie's arm a final pat. "Daphne, you can stop hiding."

"Daphne's not—"

"Don't you lie to me. I'll leave and save you both the embarrassment. I have a lunch date with Ginger. But you better tell me the next time something big happens or I won't be nearly as understanding. I'm just hoping Ginger didn't know. She couldn't have, right? I mean…" Monica was still talking as she moved into the hallway and Lettie pushed the door closed behind her.

Daphne reappeared, twisting the bottom of her white blonde hair around her finger. "She's not completely wrong."

"You mean I'm a grown woman and I can deal with a slight hiccup in my plans without melting down?"

"And that you're not as fragile as you think you are." Daphne shrugged. "Listen, I'm starving. I was thinking I'd go grab something to eat, and since you aren't going to charge me rent, I can probably handle most of the moving."

"You're an angel."

"Ban-shee." Daphne emphasized each syllable. "Don't worry. You'll get it one day." She winked.

Lettie was thankful for her best friend and glad to have the stress of moving off her plate. Daphne could be a bit of a mess, but when she wanted something she moved fast and swift. She'd probably have half her stuff moved in by the end of the day.

And to be fair, their old apartment was gross, and did smell like farts no matter what they did.

-CHAPTER EIGHT-

HER HAPPINESS AT not moving faded, however, when she heard Daphne on the phone with her brother. The thought of Lorne handling all her breakables and vintage furniture made her eye twitch. But whatever. She was letting go. Being chill.

And besides, she had her definitely not a date, but scheduled dinner, with Chandler which occupied her mind more than she wanted it to. She brushed her hair and debated lipstick before finally leaving to head towards the dining room.

But as soon as she stepped into the hallway the doorknob of Chandler's apartment turned, as though the gorgon had been listening for her. When she opened the door, her eyes were wide, the coils of her hair tight. All the things Lettie had learned to watch out for as a child.

"Come here," Chandler said, glancing down the hallway and Lettie's stomach knotted in a way she really wished it wouldn't. Even worse

Chandler's arm darted out, her fingers wrapping around Lettie's wrist, and she yanked Lettie into her apartment.

"What the hell?" Lettie's heart pounded in her chest.

"So, here's the thing," Chandler's eyes flashed, first hard stone then glittering green, and Lettie pressed her back into the door. "I didn't tell my mom I was staying here. I may have implied I had things to deal with in Atlanta before I moved back."

"What the hell?" Lettie repeated. "Chandler…Shit." Laughter bubbled in her throat. "Why? It's a small town." There was still a wildness in Chandler's eyes. The lost girl, always running. Always looking for something. The part of her Lettie had wanted so badly to soothe when she was younger.

"Lettie, I…" Chandler let out a breath and stepped closer.

"Why did you pull me in here?" Lettie's voice came out hoarse.

"I don't know." Chandler stepped back, bracing her hand on the wall and the wood crackled, turning to stone and back. "Do you still want dinner?"

"If we're not going to fight, yeah." Lettie tried to smile, to keep things light.

"My therapist says I'm combative." The wood underneath Chandler's hand continued to crackle, and she didn't move, keeping Lettie trapped in the entryway.

"Oh." Lettie didn't know what to say. She glanced at Chandler's hand. "You still do that. I…I try not to use mine anymore."

Chandler's hand dropped like the wall was hot. "Not usually. Not without meaning to. But what do you mean? You don't use your magic?"

Lettie shook her head. The entryway was so small. She'd never noticed before. "Not never, but not as much as I could. It's easier now. It's gotten smaller." Except lately it had been growing again.

Chandler took another step towards Lettie. There was barely any space between them at all. Her eyes had returned to the normal green. "Your magic isn't small."

"You don't know me well enough to say." Lettie wanted out of this apartment, out of the entryway. Just out. Because her magic was surging, filling her chest, swirling through her veins. And at that moment Chandler was right, it wasn't small at all.

Chandler seemed to misread the panic in Lettie's eyes. "Let's get out of here. Come on." She tried to move past Lettie, but Lettie put her arm up, blocking Chandler's path.

"What is this? You came back, and you were so angry. And now…What is this?"

"I don't know, but I can't breathe in this apartment. Coming back here seemed like the only thing to do, but I'm drowning, and I need air."

Lettie was about to agree, she'd opened her mouth to do just that, but the sound of heels clicked up the hallway outside the door. She knew that gait. "My mom already ambushed me earlier. I think she sent yours." News moved fast in Lilac Lake, but between Monica and Ginger it was lightning speed. The two of them were inseparable, they always had been, just like their mothers before them.

"Come on." This time Chandler didn't wait for an answer, she grabbed Lettie by the wrist and pulled her deeper into the apartment. It was strange to see the change inside, a mixture of Everly's things and Chandler's mess was strewn about the apartment, including an exceptionally large nude Lettie was sure had never belonged to Everly.

"What are you doing?" she asked as Ginger knocked on the door.

"Shh." Chandler let go of Lettie and put her fingers to her lips, then pushed the window open. She crawled halfway out the window before turning back. "You coming?"

But all Lettie could see was Chandler at eighteen, in her tiny shorts and her leather jacket, perched exactly the same in Lettie's childhood window. *I can't stop thinking about you, Letts.*

Ginger knocked on the front door again, and Chandler motioned for Lettie to come. And like she had every time Chandler had shown up, Lettie followed.

The air outside was cool, and she wished she had brought a jacket, but she chased after Chandler as she raced past the cabins and towards the lake.

Chandler didn't stop moving until the Stone and Sorcery Lodge was out of view. The lake was huge, jutting out then twisting back, a snaking shoreline that was mostly undeveloped. When Chandler finally turned towards Lettie, her face was red, but she was laughing.

"I can't believe I did that." She braced her hands on her knees, breathing heavily. "But our moms, they were never like us."

That much was true. They had both realized it when they were little. Ginger had been prom queen, Monica had been head cheerleader. They'd fit in. But was it true now? Chandler hadn't wanted to fit in, she'd skipped school and bummed cigarettes and stolen bottles of liquor. But Lettie had found her place, she had friends here, a life.

Only hours ago, she had left when Chandler got too close. But maybe her mother was right. Maybe she wasn't so fragile. And maybe she needed to learn to deal with whatever it was about Chandler that made her feel out of control, because sneaking out of windows and running down the lakeshore might make her feel seventeen again, but she wasn't, she was grown, and she had a business to run.

She pushed thoughts of what would happen after six months out of her mind. All bringing that up ever did was make Chandler mad. Better to endear herself to the gorgon, then whatever happened, at least Chandler wouldn't do it out of spite.

"You know your mom isn't going to drop this, right? She had lunch with my mom. They're going to scheme. I'm sure that's why she showed up," Lettie said, turning towards the lake. The cotton white clouds overhead reflected in the still water. She could feel the hum of magic, the pull towards the center. Not the same heady feeling as the song of the sirens but something different, deeper, something in her bones.

Chandler must have felt it too because she moved closer to the water's edge, leaving footprints on the shore. "I missed this most of all." They were both quiet for a minute, contemplating the lake. "Hey, Lettie?"

Lettie turned towards Chandler, with her unruly dark curls and her big green eyes and sharp cheekbones. The opposite of Lettie and her strawberry blonde hair, her brown eyes, her soft face that made people want to trust her. "What?"

"You can't forget about your magic. That's what I learned when I was out there. I wanted so hard to just be human. I wanted to rip out that cold center of me and be someone else. But no amount of booze, or women, or pretending I was something else changed it. I dreamed of this lake. I dreamed of you. All the time."

"Chandler, you can't say things like that to me. I know you don't mean them."

The smile fell off her face. "What?"

"I worshiped you. I would have followed you anywhere. And you didn't want me. And I know you're back and…and I want us to get along. I do. I really do. But that girl has been gone for a long time. And even if she wasn't, you never wanted her. Two months of me and you ran away. And I want us to work together. I want you to love the Lodge, and I'll climb out of as many windows as you want, but I can't be that girl again."

A muscle twitched in Chandler's jaw and the grass near the tree line rustled as something slithered through it. "Okay. But can I just show you one thing?"

"Sure." Lettie's speech hadn't released the knot in her stomach like she'd hoped it would, only coiled it tighter.

Chandler turned and walked a few steps and then reached down, plucking the snake out of the grass and draped it around her shoulders. The thing practically purred, happy just to be near her. "For years I couldn't do it. They wouldn't let me touch them. I had to accept my magic."

"You've got snakes tattooed on your arms." Lettie pointed out. She didn't mention how the arms were more muscular than they had been in high school, how adulthood fit Chandler and every lanky inch of her had grown into something beautiful.

"Well, that was part of the acceptance, and part of a bottle of whiskey and a girlfriend who was a tattoo artist."

"Was that the one who broke your heart?" Lettie followed Chandler away from the water's edge and sat in the grass, dragging her fingers across the blades. They curled towards her palm. Was Chandler right? Would she be happier if she accepted her magic?

Chandler settled into the grass and sat beside Lettie, releasing the snake back onto the ground, but it didn't go far. "No, that one ended okay, it was never serious. But Lettie, the earth loves your magic, look at it move." She was right, Lettie could feel the song in the grass, the whisper in the wind.

"Why did you leave?" Lettie didn't mean to ask the question, but it came out all the same, seeming to thicken the air around them.

Chandler leaned back, resting her head in her hands, and looking up at the sky. The clouds moved across the sky on a quick wind, puffy white giving way to gray. The day was turning dreary around them. "I was just a kid. I was scared."

"Scared of what?" Lettie studied Chandler, the loose hairs blowing across her face, the turn of her nose. Once so familiar, she had become just a memory. It was odd to have her back and even harder to find a space for her to fit in Lettie's life.

Chandler caught Lettie watching her and smiled. "Come on. Don't make me say it. You were there too."

"Scared of what, Chandler?" The blades of grass curled away from her and across the lake thunder rumbled.

Chandler straightened her neck, looking back up at the sky. "It's going to rain."

"I don't melt." Lettie laid back too, her shoulder against Chandler's, and she could feel the heat of her through her shirt, a contrast to the dark magic that emanated from her, pressing against the shimmery surge inside of Lettie.

"If we add little patios to the cabins, I think it would draw visitors. They could sit out and see the lake. Maybe we could get a few canoes. The island is the biggest draw. And we can play up the gorgon thing. They know we don't have snakes for hair or whatever else, but some statues, a snake motif."

"Okay." The idea wasn't bad, and Lettie wasn't pushy enough to force the subject. Besides, it wasn't like the question had kept her up at night. But she knew it would now. She'd spent eleven years getting over Chandler, and all it had taken was a week and she felt like she was sinking. There was more she wanted to ask. What would happen in six months? What was her plan? Did she even want the Lodge? Had she really dreamed about Lettie?

But the thing she couldn't forget about Chandler was that she was a wanderer. She was always looking towards the horizon, towards the next thing. And Lettie wasn't. She was constant, a hometown girl. What could there be but heartbreak?

Still, she let her fingers drift down until her knuckles brushed against Chandler's skin. She could feel her turn towards her, feel the weight of her gaze, but Lettie didn't turn her head.

The thunder rumbled closer to them, waves kicking up across the lake, and the sky opened.

-CHAPTER NINE-

RAIN POURED, DRENCHING them in seconds.

Chandler was the first off the ground, and she pulled Lettie with her. For a moment they ran, then Lettie stopped, still clutching Chandler's hand.

"What's the point," she asked, tipping her head towards the sky. Water coated her eyelashes and dripped down her nose.

"It's freezing!" Chandler said, tugging on her fingers. "Lettie, come on. *Please.*" She tried to run, pulling on Lettie again, and Lettie tugged back. But the grass was slick, the ground turning to mud, and Lettie slipped.

She tried to let go of Chandler, her free arm pinwheeling out, trying to catch her balance. But it was too late, she was off balance. And they both went down.

Chandler landed on Lettie, only managing not to crush her by taking the impact on her hands. Her body pressed into Lettie's, and something flashed in her eyes, but it wasn't stone.

"Lettie," she said, shifting just enough that it sent warmth flooding through Lettie, right to her core.

Words. She needed words to come out of her mouth. But she barely knew how to breathe.

Lightning struck nearby and thunder followed, loud and too close, and the moment was broken. They jumped up and ran again until the Lodge was in view.

"Not the front door," Lettie said. She couldn't walk through the entry like this, not when she was sure guests were eating their dinner.

"Shit, my window is still open," Chandler said. "Guess that's how we're going in."

"I suppose it makes up for all the times you climbed through my window," Lettie teased.

They headed for the side of the building, and Chandler scrambled halfway in before turning to pull Lettie after her. Apparently, those muscled arms weren't just for show.

Lettie dropped onto the floor and turned to make a joke to Chandler, but she was shivering. Her hair was soaked, and her teeth were chattering.

Lettie didn't think, she waved her hand, and sparkling green magic filled the hearth and the fire sprang to life, burning strong. The first real magic she'd done in years. "Oh." She brought her dirty hand to her mouth.

Chandler turned towards her grinning. "Thank you."

The magic was simple, something her mother did all the time. And Lettie wanted to say it was nothing, small and insignificant. But it had come from her. *And it had felt good.* For years she'd been so terrified, worried if she used her magic something would explode, that she'd hurt someone, but nothing bad had happened at all. Her magic had worked just as she'd wanted it to, and some of the pressure that always seemed to sit in her chest was gone.

"You're welcome," Lettie said, looking down at the mess of her clothes. "But I should go."

"You could stay," Chandler said, peeling her wet jacket off. "You're only going across the hall." She kicked off her dirty shoes and moved closer to Lettie.

A week. A week was all it took to turn Lettie's life upside down. "I don't think I should. We have to work together."

Chandler glanced down, her tongue darting out and wetting her bottom lip. The firelight illuminated her in the dark apartment, making all her sharp features even sharper. When she looked up, she caught Lettie's gaze in her own. "We don't have to think about that."

Didn't they? Lettie did. "Chandler, this is my life. I know it's just a season for you, but this is all I've ever wanted."

"Fine." She stepped back, making space for Lettie to leave. For her to be the one to walk away this time. "Just business then."

And each step was heavy, but the door wasn't far.

Lettie didn't know how long she stood with her forehead on the apartment door, her eyes closed, her heart pounding. She prayed the apartment was empty. She didn't want to explain any of this to Daphne. She didn't even know how to explain it to herself.

Finally, she went inside, and the shower was hot. Dark, dirty water swirled down the drain. She tried to keep her mind clear, but it was an impossible task.

So instead of thinking about Chandler, she thought about the Lodge. She thought of the changes she would make and the things she would keep the same. She imagined how it would be in the summer, the cabins full of guests, the lake sparkling in the sun.

And eventually the water ran cold, and Lettie stepped out of the shower, surveying the dirty clothes strewn across the floor. A problem for later. She needed to go back to her other apartment because that's where her clothes were, which unfortunately meant she was going to have to wear something out of her grandmother's closet.

She wrapped a towel around herself and pushed open the door, only to come face to face with her brother. "Lorne!" Her favorite antique vase was cradled in his arms.

"Hey." He looked at a spot above her head. "Daphne asked me to help move all your stuff. I had the day off and figured you do just about everything for me, so I'd start on it."

So much for going back to her place. "Oh. Well, thanks." She clutched the towel to her chest.

"Amelia just put some clothes in your room." He was still staring above her head. "Daphne's grabbing some stuff from the truck. Are you…can you put some clothes on?"

"Like you aren't shirtless all the goddamn time." She pushed past him and towards the master bedroom. Part of Lettie wished Daphne had let her pack her own clothes, she hated to think of Amelia going through her things, but she had been planning on wearing her dead grandma's clothes, so she supposed it was all for the best.

All her clothes were strewn across the bed. Allowing Daphne to spearhead moving was a sign of just how busy she was. Of course, she had jumped right in, not taking time to plan just grabbing things. Lettie took a deep breath, determined to let it go. She'd known Daphne was doing this, she'd known Lorne was involved which would inevitably mean Amelia was involved, so what right did she have to get her feathers ruffled now?

She would have to follow up with their landlord though, something she was sure Daphne hadn't thought of in all the commotion. She heard her friend's voice come out of the living room followed by the laughter of her brother. Two chaos goblins that she couldn't imagine life without.

So, for once, she really did let it go. Her things would be moved. She'd deal with the finer details later. But she had the Lodge, she had a new, spacious apartment, and people who loved her enough to move her things on a few hours' notice. She wasn't going to sweat the small things. It was time to start working on a new Lettie, a more mature, business owning Lettie who knew how to delegate and who totally wasn't hung up on her super annoying high school ex.

She grabbed a pair of leggings and a gray shirt and pulled them on. She caught sight of herself in the mirror and paused.

She looked like the same old Lettie, but she had done magic. Simple, everyday magic, but real magic. Not just the flowers and vines that curled towards her but a choice. *Fire.*

And she was fine. Everything was fine. Maybe she really was a brand-new Lettie. Maybe, and she hated to admit it, her mother was right—she wasn't fragile.

"What are you smiling at?" Amelia asked, coming into the bedroom with a lamp under her arm.

"Oh…nothing. I'm just happy to be here. It feels right."

"Well, I hope so, because I don't want to move all this back." She grinned. "I'm just bringing the essentials though. Daphne booked actual movers for the big things in two days. I was nosy though and wanted to see this place."

Movers? Well, that was something. "It's kind of sudden, but—"

"But it's like twice as big and way nicer? Yeah, I would have done the same thing." She put the lamp down. "Plus, you grew up here. I slept on an air mattress in the apartment above the bar for a month when I first bought it."

"Speaking of your bar, how do you do it? I've been excited my whole life to run this place, but now it's real and it's a lot. I've been kind of putting off any major decisions because it runs itself after all these years but it's *mine*. My responsibility."

Amelia pushed Lettie's clothes to the side and sat on the bed, her red hair cascading over her shoulder. "I know what you mean. I kind of impulse bought the bar when I saw it for sale. And it was fun and exciting for like two days, and then it was like 'oh shit I have a business.' But that's the thing—*you* have it. And you're like me, you love this town. And now you own a little piece of it. So, yeah, it's hard, and times can get lean, but then you'll step back, and you'll look at what you've done, and you'll be proud."

"I hope so." Lettie pulled at the hem of her shirt just so she had something to do with her hands. "I don't want to ruin it."

"Lettie, be serious. You aren't going to ruin it. You've got more drive in your pinkie than Hattie and Everly ever did. How many months did they spend in the Caribbean each year? I loved them both, but life was a game for them. You're exactly what this place needs."

"God, I'm so gloomy lately." Lettie grabbed a hair clip and twisted her hair up. "Maybe I'll take up residence at the bar, be one of those sad day drinkers."

"Yeah. I'm sure this is totally a long-term problem and not the result of seeing your ex for the first time in over a decade. Alcoholism is *definitely* the solution."

"Fucking small towns." Lettie sat on the bed beside her. "Can't shit without a write up in the paper."

"Gross. But you might remember my little melt down a few years back when Laura left."

Lettie tried to suppress a chuckle and failed miserably, earning her a scowl from Amelia. "I mean…who hasn't accidentally set their own lawn on fire?"

"See, you've got a long way to go before rock bottom." Amelia clapped her on the back. "Looks like the rain is starting to let up. Come on, manual labor will help you feel better."

As it turned out, Amelia was right. And she felt better surrounded by a mixture of her things and her grandmothers, like Hattie was watching over her, approving of her taking over the Lodge.

Later that night, she stood in the doorway to the kitchen, watching Daphne as she watched TV, her feet in Lorne's lap, her head against the armrest.

"Move," she said, nudging her brother and he scooted closer to Daphne. "Thanks for today."

He shrugged. "That's what brothers are for. But are you going to use Gran's bed? I was thinking if you weren't—"

"You can have her bed frame," she said, dodging a slap from Daphne.

"Stop giving our things away. And be quiet, I can't hear," Daphne said, trying to sit up, but Lorne closed his arms around her legs.

"No violence," he chided. "And they're my things too. She was my grandma. You're the one living here for free."

"You're an idiot." Daphne grabbed the remote from the coffee table and turned the TV up.

Trying to be subtle, Lettie nudged the papers strewn across the coffee table with her foot. A college header was at the top, applications for a master's program. She smiled to herself and settled deeper into the couch without saying anything, full of pride for her best friend.

-CHAPTER TEN-

"I LIKE THIS one," Pepper said, looking over the paint samples Lettie had gotten for the cabins. The color she was pointing at was a beautiful green, a few shades lighter than the lake.

"It's my favorite too," Lettie told her, sweeping all the samples back into a pile. The movers had come and gone. She'd come to an agreement with her landlord, and now it was time to get to the actual work.

Which would have Lettie excited—if a little nervous—except Chandler hadn't said more than a dozen words to her in the last few days. And half of those had been while they were signing the final papers with Hillchamp.

One step forward, two steps back. Whatever. *You can only control yourself.* She liked to imagine that's what her therapist would say if she had one.

But there were choices to be made, and they'd need to dip into their shared business expense account. So, whether Chandler liked it or not, she was going to have to talk to Lettie.

"Think she'll cooperate?" Lettie asked, gathering her papers.

"Only one way to find out, and I don't intend to be in the middle." Pepper shooed her away and Lettie took the hint.

She had been trying to forget the day they had run from Chandler's mother and gotten trapped in a downpour. Lettie had hoped they might be turning a corner, but now things were back to how they were before—tense and awkward. But she could deal with that more easily than open hostility.

The Lodge was quiet as she pushed open the door to the apartment's hallway and knocked three times on Chandler's door. Oak's face appeared in the doorway.

"Hey. I was just about to go," they said, glancing over their shoulder.

"You don't have to," Lettie said. In fact, she'd appreciate having a buffer.

"Gotta work," they clarified, but they pushed the door open and yelled into the apartment, "Chan, it's Lettie and I'm letting her in."

Even more of Chandler's aesthetic was visible in the apartment now, and the smell of Everly was slowly dissipating, replaced with the earthy scent of Chandler.

"What was—?" Chandler stopped, her eyes wide. Dark magic sparked at her side, and the air in front of her smoldered with it. "Shit! Lettie!" She was in a sports bra, her tattoos on full display, and her hair frizzing out where it came loose from her ponytail.

"Sorry, I didn't mean to intrude." Lettie tried to avert her eyes, but her traitorous retinas kept moving back to Chandler and the drops of sweat running down her neck. "I can come back."

"No, it's fine." Chandler grabbed a hoodie off of the back of her couch and put it on. "What's up?"

"I'm…yeah, I'm going to go," Oak said and rushed out of the apartment. So much for a buffer.

"The contractor needs us to make some decisions about the cabins. I want to get a few done so we can get pictures to put up on the website," Lettie said.

"You can pick whatever you want." Chandler shrugged, turning around to walk into the kitchen. She made another noncommittal gesture and opened the fridge.

Her shorts were very short. Not that Lettie was looking. "Come on, are you really going to be like this just because I didn't want to sleep with you?"

Chandler spun around, a water bottle dangling from her fingers. "*Excuse me?* Sleep with you? I didn't even touch you, I asked if you wanted to stay. I was trying to be friendly, and you shut that down and let me know we're just business partners. If I wanted to fuck you, you would know."

Lettie tried her best not to pull a face. "Come on, Chandler. I've been on the receiving end of this before."

"Oh, yes." She twisted the top of the bottle and tossed it. The lid clattered across the counter to land near Lettie, solid stone. Well, this was going well. "I slept with you once when I was a teenager. Now you know me so well? I guess you've got me all figured out. I'm thirty years old, Lettie. You have no idea who I am now."

Lettie opened her mouth but realized anything that came out of it was going to be all wrong. So, she shut it and counted to three. If Chandler didn't leave in six months, they could be working together for years. They could not keep fighting. "I'm sorry. I shouldn't have assumed." Though she didn't think she was mistaken, but that was her personal business to keep in her head.

"Fine. Hand over the folder and I'll look through it." Chandler pulled her hair out of its ponytail. Unbrushed, Lettie could see where the tales came from, it curled into thick coils that snaked around her face and over her shoulders.

For a few minutes Chandler was silent, her eyebrows scrunched together, her mouth occasionally moving to mouth the words she read. "I like it. Seriously. It's good stuff, Lettie. You've got an eye for this."

"Anything to add? There are cheaper options, but I think quality is worth the money." Lettie leaned on the counter by Chandler, looking over the sketches and price quotes.

Chandler chewed her lip and nodded. "That's fine. Stone and Sorcery isn't cheap. That's not what you want."

"Or you," Lettie offered.

"Or me," Chandler said, not meeting Lettie's eyes. "Do you want a beer?" She straightened up, pushing the folder away from her.

"Um…sure. But are you okay with the colors? And we're going to try to keep all the original flooring. If that's okay."

Chandler shoved a beer in Lettie's direction and took a long drink of her own. "I like this one." She pointed to the same color Pepper had picked out. "I think you should add some more activities between the cabins and the lake. A fire pit, some cornhole, things to bring people out and give them something to do other than swim. And maybe you— we—should repaint the outside of the Lodge to a darker shade of green. Then we can get the kayaks in the same color. We could put the logo on the sides. Free advertisement for anyone else on the lake."

"We'd need a logo."

"And an updated website. I can handle that." Chandler finished the rest of her beer and tossed the empty into the trash before fishing another one out of the fridge.

Lettie almost told her to slow down. Take it easy. But she bit that back, filing it away with all the other things she wanted to say but didn't. "I remember you used to draw."

"Still do sometimes." Chandler leaned back against the counter. "I can make some sketches. I have a few ideas. A little snake, some flowers."

"That sounds great." Lettie grinned. "Hey, are you hungry? I was thinking of going to Hershel's for dinner."

"I am hungry, but I cannot eat another burger and fries. I need a vegetable. What about The Glass Fox? My treat."

"That would be nice." Probably a disaster waiting to happen, but potentially nice to get along. She finished her beer. "Meet in twenty?"

"What? You don't like my outfit?" Chandler did a little shimmy, the already short shorts riding up dangerously high. "Yeah, twenty works. And sorry I snapped."

"Your therapist says you're combative." Lettie winked and headed across the hall before Chandler could respond to find Daphne sitting in the bay window. "Do I look okay?"

"In general, yes. For something specifically, it depends."

"A business dinner." She tried to keep her face neutral.

"No." Daphne stood up shaking her head. "You are not getting dinner with her, Letts. Bad idea."

"She's my business partner. And you've got to let it go. All of that was so long ago. Please." She templed her fingers together, mock begging. "Help me pick something out?"

The words were Daphne's kryptonite. "Fine. I'll help you pick out clothes, but I'm not getting over it. I have never let anything go in my entire life. I am a tiny vessel of hatred and I have no intention of changing."

"I know, and I love you for it." Lettie led Daphne to her room, then sat on her bed. There was no need to help. Whatever she picked, Daphne's choice would be better.

"Do you want to be, like, business casual, or do you wanna make her gag? In a good way," she added at the look on Lettie's face.

"Business, I guess." Lettie grabbed a brush from her vanity and set to work on her hair.

"Wrong." Daphne turned around and looked Lettie over. "You, my beautiful best friend, are going to make her rue the day."

"Rue what day, Daph?"

"All of them." She grabbed clothes from the closet, holding them up then putting them back before she settled on an outfit. A little black sundress, tights and a denim jacket. Simple, but flattering and not trying too hard.

Twenty minutes later, Daphne had brushed makeup across Lettie's face, and forced her into heels, despite Lettie's protests.

"Should I…I don't know? I'm nervous. Why am I nervous?" Lettie yanked at the bottom of her jacket.

"Fuck if I know. She's the one who should be nervous." Daphne pulled Lettie away from the mirror and pushed her towards the door. "Unless you want to stand her up. That might be fun."

"You're a horrible influence."

"You're welcome." Daphne gave her another shove. "Have fun. Don't do anything I wouldn't do."

She hurried through the Lodge, grinning at the few guests that milled around. Once she got to the porch, she took a moment and a deep breath.

She needed to get control of herself, contain the way her heartbeat, though she didn't know if it was in anticipation of the verbal sparring match she was sure to find herself in, or something else entirely.

But Chandler was right, she was no longer the teenager Lettie had known. And while Lettie still found her abrasive and short-tempered, she thought maybe, one day, they could be good business partners. After all, their grandmothers had been best friends, and their moms adored each other. There had to be some common ground between them.

Also, they basically lived together, and it was weird, and would only get worse if they fought all the time. Lettie had had no reservations about moving into her grandmother's old apartments, that had always been the plan. The apartment felt more like home than anywhere else in the world but having the girl she'd been in love with as a teenager, and who she was tentatively trying and failing to build a friendship with, across the hall was something else entirely.

Something that made Lettie feel things she didn't want to feel. And she knew it was unfair, that Chandler had as much right to the Lodge as she did, but she wished she was still far away, away from the Lodge, away from Lettie and her thoughts. Just away, doing whatever she'd been doing.

The door opened, and Chandler stepped out. She had on her standard outfit, tight jeans, a plain t-shirt, and a leather jacket, but she'd finished off the look with heeled boots and gold jewelry. Her hair was the same as it had been earlier, still tightly coiled, as thought it was just as tense as Lettie felt. Chandler's eyes flashed at the sight of Lettie, and something moved in the bushes, making Lettie jump.

Two snakes, wound together until she couldn't tell where one ended and the other began, sat at the foot of the stairs. Not that there weren't other Gorgons in Lilac Lake, there were, but none of them seemed to exude as much magic as Chandler. Lettie could feel it like a magnet, pulling her towards the woman and apparently the snakes could too.

"I'll get my car," Chandler said, rummaging through her purse. "Don't want to get caught in the rain again."

Lettie stiffened, but Chandler was smiling as she hurried down the porch and towards the back of the Lodge, serpents at her heels.

A business dinner. Just a business dinner. Lettie kept saying it to herself. And she wanted it to be. The last thing she wanted to feel for Chandler was anything more than a light friendship. She needed to go out later, get Lorne to drive her a few towns over and find someone—anyone—to take her mind off Chandler.

Chandler pulling around in a candy apple red sports car didn't help. She rolled down the window and leaned out of the side. "Better than the old beater from high school, right?"

"Oh my god, I'd forgotten about that thing." Lettie pulled the door open and slid in.

"Ended up catching on fire. I made the local news." Chandler stretched her arm across the back of the seat, turning to back out of the driveway, and bringing her face awfully close to Lettie's. The scent of earth after a rain filled her nose.

"This looks pricey. What were you doing before you moved here?" Though Lettie had known Chandler's earlier comments were true, the weight of them hit her like bricks in her stomach. She didn't know anything about her at all.

"I worked in development. I did alright. I got myself this as a gift after landing a huge sale."

"Oh." Lettie didn't know what to say. What was Chandler doing back here? She had a whole life outside of Lilac Lake. Lettie kept thinking of the future, of how life would be years from now, once the animosity had died and they were working together. But would there be years? She still had no idea what Chandler was planning to do once the terms of their grandmother's contract was up, but she doubted it was staying here.

Lilac Lake was just a resting place for Chandler. So, Lettie would keep on working and try not to stress. Whatever Chandler did for a living, Lettie was sure she'd enjoy a bit of passive income. And if they could be friendly, Lettie could offer to run the place and Chandler could still get a cut of the profits. It was a good deal, and now that Chandler wasn't at her throat, maybe it was something she would take Lettie up on.

They pulled into the parking lot of the Glass Fox, and Chandler turned the car off. "Letts?" She turned in her seat.

"Yeah?" The car was small and seemingly growing smaller. Lettie longed to fling the door open, but Chandler held her in her gaze.

"I really am sorry. Leaving was the right thing to do, but I shouldn't have done it like that."

Lettie shrugged. "Like you said, we were kids." She'd spent the whole fall of her senior year dreaming of this moment, of Chandler coming home. But now ten years had passed, and she didn't expect the mix of emotions that swelled inside of her. "Why wouldn't you talk to me though? Like, ever? Even when you came back to visit."

Chandler chewed her lip. "Let's get food. Then we can talk, I promise."

"Okay," Lettie said, eager to be out of the car. She pushed the door open and inhaled the crisp air. Somewhere nearby someone was having a bonfire, and the rich aroma filled her nose. She steadied herself and followed Chandler inside.

It was the off season and there was no wait at the restaurant. The hostess led them to a little table set for two, tucked away near a window. She'd forgotten how romantic The Glass Fox was when it wasn't full of people dripping from the lake and reeking of sunscreen.

"Evening. Oh, hey, Lettie." The waiter was a friend of Lorne's, Gestin Page. They'd played football together in high school. He looked between the two of them, a smirk pulling at his mouth.

Lettie contemplated stomping his foot. She'd never liked him much, but she'd liked very few of Lorne's friends besides Amelia. "Can we get a bottle of chardonnay?"

"Absolutely. Let me know if you have any questions about the menu."

Gestin left, and the only thing between Chandler and Lettie was flickering candlelight. Lettie knew she should say something, but instead she opened the menu, hiding her face behind it until Gestin came back, pouring a glass for each of them.

She ordered eggplant parmesan and Chandler got the veal saltimbocca. And then there was no menu, nothing to hold between them.

Chandler toyed with her napkin on the table, then looked up at Lettie with those eyes, so big and green. Lettie had never found a way not to fall into them. "Do you really not use your magic anymore?"

The question threw her off balance. She hadn't been expecting it. "It's not like I *never* use it. I just…it's safe this way."

"You shouldn't hide yourself." Chandler took a sip of her drink. "I saw the way you looked when you lit that fire. It had been a while."

Who was she to tell Lettie how to live, after all these years? "Come on. It's not like you use yours all the time."

Chandler's eyes flashed, growing pale, before returning to normal. "Because I'm not a witch. I've heard you and the others—shifters, fae, all of you—I hear the way they talk about magic, the way it warms you. Mine isn't like that, Lettie. My magic is a cold pit."

"I didn't—" She'd heard it before too, the way the supes in her town talked about their magic. But had she ever really thought about it before? Her magic, as much as it frightened her, was warm and bright. Even at her worst, she'd never described it as a cold pit.

"Gorgon magic is only meant to hurt. The only good is the snakes, and some people would call that debatable as far as being good. I can't do the things you do. I can turn things to stone—people if I'm not careful. And even the snakes, I can feel the way they'd do what I want. They'd attack for me. Does that sound like your magic?"

"No," Lettie admitted. "But we blew up town square, Chandler. We could have killed someone, and that wasn't all you. Does your magic do that?"

"No. And that's why I left." She glanced down at her nearly empty glass of wine and reached for the bottle to refill it, but Lettie caught her hand, covering it with her own.

"You were scared?" She'd known it, deep down she'd known it, but there was always a voice in the back of her head saying she wasn't enough. She hadn't been enough for Chandler to stay. She hadn't had enough magic to save her father. An ignorant thought, she wasn't a doctor. Even so, it lingered.

"Of course, I was scared. I was…" She sighed and took another long drink of her wine and Lettie worried she was driving Chandler to alcoholism. "You and I never figured out a way to get along. And it almost blew up the town."

"We got along," Lettie insisted.

"No, we didn't. We made out on Siren Island and—well, you know what we did. But we *never* got along."

"Do you think we can now?" Lettie couldn't bear to look directly at those green eyes while she waited for an answer, so instead she looked out the window, where the sun was sinking lower in the sky. The town spread out before her, bathed in golden light, and she had to force herself to turn back to Chandler. "Listen, we can go over this forever. Let's just try to get along now."

"About the six-month stipulation—"

Lettie put her hand up, cutting her off. "Let's just cross that bridge when we get to it. I think before we make any decisions we need to see if we can make this work. If we can be partners."

Chandler's response was cut off by the waiter returning. The smirk was still on his lips, though he did his best to hide it, and she had no doubt Lorne would hear about her night.

She smiled sweetly at Gestin. "I heard Alice was asking about you at The Three Sisters."

"Really?" He slid her plate onto the table, his smirk replaced by a bright hopefulness. He'd always had a crush on Alice.

"Nope." Lettie's smile turned to a glare. "And you better not tell my brother I'm here."

"You're mean, you know that?"

"I like her mean," Chandler said, looking at him with curiosity. "Didn't we graduate together? Oh, I remember you!"

Gestin's cheeks turned red, and Lettie almost felt sorry for him. He hadn't really done anything wrong. Lorne was his friend, of course he'd tell him if he saw Lettie. But there was something about his smirk, a reminder of what the town thought when they saw the two of them together, that irked her. As much as the citizens of Lilac Lake were like family to Lettie there were some things you never lived down and explosions tended to be one of them.

"We'll take another basket of bread," Chandler said. She lifted her glass as Gestin left. "To figuring out how the fuck to be friends."

Lettie clinked her glass against Chandler's. "And you think the answer might be at the bottom of one of these glasses?"

"I think I'm suddenly remembering I'm in my hometown, I've got a Lodge to take care of, my ex is sitting across from me, and I've never had good coping skills."

"Yeah, me either." Lettie said, grabbing her fork.

-CHAPTER ELEVEN-

GESTIN WAS NOTHING but professional the rest of the meal, and Lettie felt guilty enough to leave a hefty tip on top of what Chandler left. Chandler had insisted on paying for the entire meal, and Lettie wasn't going to argue. Buying out her old lease had taken a good chunk of her bank account.

When she finally stood and made her way into the moonlit night, Lettie's feet were wobbly, and Chandler wasn't much better.

Chandler fished around in her purse and then stopped. "I shouldn't drive."

"We can walk," Lettie said. She had sold her car a few years ago. She couldn't justify the payment when she could make it across the entire town in half an hour.

"Oh, Lettie," Chandler was drunker than she was, and she looped her arm through Lettie's. "I swore I'd never move back here, but now that I'm here it's harder to ignore all the things I missed. I'm so tired of pretending."

What was she pretending? Lettie didn't have the courage to ask.

"Come here." Lettie pulled on her arm. The temperature had dropped, and wind whipped through the town. Chandler followed as they made their way out of the side road and onto Main Street. She could hear voices from across the square, people laughing inside The Three Sisters.

The air was chilled without the sun to warm it, and she pulled Chandler closer. Further from the bar the town was quiet without the rumble of cars down the street.

Arm in arm, they walked the few steps to the open center of town. In the spring and summer there would be farmer's markets and festivals, couples sitting on the benches beneath the fairy lights hung from the streetlamps, but now it was deserted.

The light above the gazebo made the bright white paint look yellow, and the bushes that surrounded the gazebo faded against the dark bricks at the base.

"What are we doing?" Chandler asked, extracting her arm from Lettie's.

"Right here," Lettie said. She still hadn't found the spot she was searching for, but she knew it was there. It had been there for eleven years. Then she found it, the bare spot in the ground where grass never grew. "Look. You're always part of the town."

God, she was drunk, or maybe it was just her nerves, the intoxication that always came from being around Chandler. She didn't know what she was trying to accomplish. Did she even want Chandler to stay? If she had to explain why she was trying to make the gorgon feel better, she didn't think she'd be able to.

Chandler made her way over to Lettie and stared down at the bare spot of dirt. Lettie had no idea what she was going to say but didn't expect her to burst into laughter the way she did. "Lettie, shut up!" She pushed her shoulder playfully.

"Huh?"

"You know what? I'm over this. So, we blew it up. Have you ever gone more than a week without hearing about it? And I bet you've done all kinds of cool things." Chandler sat down on the gazebo steps and patted the spot next to her. "And so have I. We're going to make Stone and Sorcery the biggest tourist spot in this stupid town and you're going to forget this happened."

Lettie sat down next to her. "I'm sorry. I know I keep bringing it up. But you're right. It was so long ago. It's just when it happened it was this huge thing, and you were gone, so it was all on me. I kept thinking how you should be there. How if you were there it would be funnier."

"It would have been. Didn't you ever want to leave? Not let this define you?"

"It didn't define me. Not like you think it did." Except she didn't do magic anymore. Every time she tried she came back to that moment. The way Chandler had been yelling, and she'd been yelling, and then

Chandler's lips had been on hers and her magic had built inside of her, a tidal wave she couldn't control. The helpless feeling of knowing something was going to happen and being unable to stop it.

And maybe she had never realized before just how much she'd let it take over her life. She'd let the doubt seep in, and she'd never bothered to wring it back out. She'd flitted from job to job, mostly working for her grandma, and trying to keep her head down so she never did something like that again.

But she was tired of keeping her head down. She was tired of trying to be small and perfect and never wrong. "I want to do terrible things. Big mistakes."

"Okay, then we're doing it." Chandler grinned and part of Lettie said that was enough. She should go home. That smile had never led her anywhere good. Trouble. Danger. Take an off ramp.

"What are we doing?"

"We're going to Siren Island."

"It's already dark."

"I heard your brother has a boat. And I bet he'd give you the keys." Chandler's grin was growing, her hair coiling tighter. She jumped up, touching one pointer finger and then the other to her nose. "I'm not that drunk, I just wasn't ready to go home. I can drive the boat for the three minutes it takes to get to the island."

This was a bad idea. Plain and simple. A terrible, terrible idea. Exactly the kind of mistake she wanted to make. "Stay here. Don't move," Lettie said, pushing herself up from the steps. "Seriously. Don't leave."

The grin faded. "I won't go anywhere."

The door of the Three Sisters beckoned her, bright and inviting, and she tried not to grin too much as she went inside. Her brother was behind the bar, his dirty blonde hair artfully askew, a grin on his face and a laughing girl in front of him.

"Lorne, do you have the keys to your boat?"

He pulled a face, a contemplative look she rarely saw him wear. "Little sister, what kind of trouble are you up to?" But when she tried to answer he cut her off. "No, don't tell me. I don't want to be an accomplice." He pulled his keyring out of his pocket, and Lettie tried to ignore the woman he had been flirting with staring at her as she extracted his boat key. "Do not sink her, Lettie. I swear to God, I love you, but I will murder you."

She pushed herself up on the bar and kissed his cheek. "Just a little midnight cruise."

"You better not tell Daph. She'll have that girl's head. But I like this. You look happy. Now go on girl, git!"

As it turned out, Chandler knew all the ins and outs of a boat. Lettie didn't ask why. She was sure there was a beautiful heiress or something behind it. Someone with a sailboat and designer clothes.

As Chandler steered the boat across the short distance between the dock and the island, Lettie rummaged around under the seats until she found a bottle of rum.

Lettie rarely drank much, a cocktail at the bar or a glass of wine with Daphne, but with Chandler she felt like a teenager again, carefree in a way she hadn't in years. And anyway, she was pushing those feelings away. She was making mistakes.

Chandler glanced back to look at her. "You okay? You're kind of pale over there, witch."

Lettie twisted the lid of the bottle and took a long drink just as the boat slowed. The liquid snaked through her body, warming her. Chandler got out first and offered Lettie her hand. The sand was soft and her feet sunk into it.

A hundred things raced through Lettie's mind, most of them involving Chandler, rose-tinged and faded memories of a golden summer. Doubts tried to creep into her mind, but she pushed them away. Not tonight. Tonight she was going to be careless. She'd earned it.

"It was this way," Chandler said, starting towards the small copse of trees near the water's edge. She grabbed the bottle from Lettie.

Overhead the moon shone on them, full and round. Lettie's heart pounded, her magic kicking up inside of her. She could feel the ancient source of her power here, something deep in the earth that called to her, but she could also feel other magic, the dark vein of something else. Powerful and grim. The thing that gave rise to the strange supes of Lilac Lake.

She stopped and ran her fingers over the bark of a tree, admiring the way the sparse leaves mottled the moonlight. When they were teenagers, Chandler had been a hurricane, a force, something that seemed unstoppable and inevitable, or maybe a riptide, a current to grab Lettie and sweep her away.

She wasn't sure anything had changed.

The island was silent, the scurry of small creatures through the underbrush the only sound to fill the night.

Taking the bottle back, she took another drink and let the rum twist with the magic in her stomach. She knew if she kept walking there was a pool, maybe three feet across, barely enough for two girls to fit inside. "It was warmer that night."

"No skinny dipping, then?" Chandler teased and then laughed loudly, breaking through the silence of the island.

Bats burst from the trees overhead and Lettie screamed, lurching forward and right into Chandler's arms. She tried to pull away, but the gorgon held tight, her leather clad arms wrapped around Lettie. The air was thick with hot, dark magic. Forbidden magic, the thing that had pulled Lettie to Chandler all those years ago, and which she still found hard to resist.

She could feel the warmth of Chandler through the fabric and heard the thump of the bottle as it fell from her hands and onto the ground below.

"I almost called so many times," Chandler said. "I wrote so many emails I never sent. And then so much time had passed I didn't know how to say what I wanted to say. I told my Nan last Christmas that I felt guilty about how things had panned out. So, this might all be my fault."

Was it the booze or just Chandler, so close, saying things she'd once wanted to hear so badly that was making Lettie's head swim? "Keep talking."

Chandler chuckled. "I'm not very good at saying things. But I wanted you to know, it was never that I didn't care. I was terrified by how much I did. I wanted to get out of here, but you made me want to stay."

Lettie's resolve was washing away. She wrapped her arms around Chandler's shoulders, tangling her fingers in the curls of her hair. "And now?"

"Now I want to kiss you, Lettie Katz."

Instead, Lettie kissed her. She pulled Chandler close, barely brushing her lips against the gorgon's but Chandler's arms tightened around her, and she deepened the kiss.

Her lips parted and her tongue swept through Lettie's mouth. Chandler grasped her by the back of her head, and Lettie ran her hands down Chandler's sides to the bottom of her shirt. She let her fingers wander beneath the fabric, brushing against Chandler's warm skin, over the ridges of her spine and the planes of her shoulder blade.

There were a million reasons not to do this, from the fact that they couldn't get along, to the business they owned together, but Chandler had always been the one thing to undo Lettie. Smart, prudent Lettie fell away when those green eyes captured her and nothing had ever changed, not the burning in her core or the want that swelled inside her chest.

Chandler moaned into her mouth, breaking apart from Lettie, her chest heaving. The night shrouded her features, but Lettie could still see those captivating eyes, earnest and wide. "I don't want you to regret—"

"I won't." Lettie cut her off with a kiss, though she knew the words weren't true. But she had so many regrets, and she would rather regret this than regret never knowing.

The words ignited Chandler, and she pushed Lettie back until she stumbled on roots, and her back pressed against the wide trunk of a tree. Chandler trapped Lettie's hands above her head, winding her fingers around her wrist. She lowered her mouth, breathing Lettie's name against her neck.

Lettie could feel the darkness of her magic as she trailed kisses down her throat. There was something inside of her, some pragmatic corner of her brain urging her to stop, that she'd been drinking and everything would be worse in the harsh light of day. Reminding her this wasn't what she did. She made the smart choice, she followed the rules.

Tonight, Lettie didn't want to listen to that voice. She pressed herself into Chandler, and her magic sparked at her fingertips, painting the night in brilliant, sparkling green.

Chandler glanced up at Lettie's hands, smiling, and let go of her wrists. Lettie rushed to take off her jacket, already missing the gorgon's touch. The night was chilly, but she didn't care. Chandler pressed a leg between her thighs, and grabbed Lettie's shirt, pulling it over her head and lowering her mouth to Lettie's throat.

Lettie let her head fall back, closing her eyes. Chandler ran her teeth down Lettie's neck, and every place their bodies touched ignited with want and magic. The gorgon was still fully dressed, and her clothed breasts moved against Lettie's, the fabric rough against her peaked nipples and she squirmed at the sensation.

"Chandler, please," she begged, though she didn't know what she was asking. Only for more. For longer. Just another moment of letting go, of being someone else, someone who leapt without looking.

Chandler grasped Lettie by the hair at the base of her neck, holding her tight, her mouth returned to Lettie's neck. She pushed her free hand between them, her nails scratching as they ran down Lettie's stomach and hooked into the waistband of her pants.

Lettie wished they weren't in the woods, that she had dragged Chandler back to her bed, where they could explore every inch of each other, but those thoughts were forgotten as Chandler's hand moved lower and her thumb brushed against Lettie's underwear. She bucked against the gorgon's hand as pleasure moved through her core, and Lettie ignited. All the magic and wildness she had kept locked away broke free. With every inch of her body on fire, she kissed Chandler fiercely, moaning into her mouth.

Bursts of green sparkled through the air, and for a moment Chandler stilled, but only long enough to breathe Lettie's name as magic danced around them, reflected in her eyes. Lettie was thankful for the tree behind her, the pressure of its bark as Chandler's fingers continued their exploration, finding their way beneath her layers of clothes and onto her skin.

Each touch felt like an apology, the years melting away. And then it felt like nothing but pleasure as Chandler slipped a finger inside her, and her thumb brushed against Lettie's clit.

Chandler's hand retreated and Lettie groaned, but Chandler spun her around and pressed her against the tree. Her body was flush against Lettie's back and her hand returned, her fingers moved expertly, without hesitation. Another finger joined the first, and the gorgon knew each spot to touch to make Lettie squirm. "I want to feel you come."

"Yes," Lettie moaned as the rhythm of Chandler's fingers increased, and she drove into her so hard the bark of the tree dug into Lettie's skin.

"Good girl." She yanked Lettie's pants down and brought her mouth closer to nip at Lettie's earlobe. "Like this?"

"Yes," Lettie repeated. Chandler's thumb circled her clit as her fingers curved and moved inside Lettie making her legs tremble. She grasped at the tree for support, breathing heavy, an orgasm building in her stomach.

Chandler's arm snaked back up, holding her steady as she fucked her relentlessly.

Lettie could feel Chandler's dark power brushing its tendrils against her skin and she let it enter her. Chandler gripped her tight and whispered in her ear, "After this I want to take you home and taste your sweet pussy. I want you exhausted."

Lettie couldn't form words, only a moan as her knees went weak. No one had spoken to her like that before and she wanted more. She pressed her ass into Chandler, and the Gorgon slammed her forward, adding a third finger to those inside of her.

She came with a scream. The only thing that kept her up was Chandler's arm around her waist. She withdrew her hand and Lettie turned to find Chandler bringing her fingers to her mouth.

And Lettie knew she was falling, without knowing what would be at the bottom, but she wanted to find out, to keep being reckless and wild. To feel alive, no longer trapped by expectation, but free to find her footing even if she wobbled.

Chandler brushed Lettie's hair behind her ear then bent down. She planted a kiss on Lettie's thighs and brushed a final touch against her clit, the singular touch almost enough to make her come again.

"Put on your clothes. I can have you in my bed in five minutes." She handed Lettie her shirt and straightened her jacket.

Lettie awoke to the smell of coffee and even more delicious memories—Chandler between her thighs, purring that she was a good girl, explaining how delicious she tasted, the way Chandler had looked above Lettie as she rode her, pressing their cores together, Chandler's fingers digging into her hips.

And the gorgon had not lied. When Lettie had finally fallen asleep, she had been exhausted in the best way, entirely spent and surprisingly not full of regret, though she was sure now, in the morning sun, it would come soon.

The door opened and Chandler came in, clutching two cups of coffee. Beautiful. Chandler was absolutely beautiful. And for now, still groggy with sleep, that was all Lettie would focus on. A beautiful woman.

Chandler sat the coffee cups on the side table and got into bed. She had on the same tiny shorts she had worn before and nothing else. Lettie reached for her, pulling her down into the sheets and capturing a pert pink nipple in her mouth.

Chandler brushed one hand against Lettie's hair, the other down her back, and when Lettie looked up, she was grinning.

"You've learned a few things while you were gone." Lettie hadn't had sex that good in a while.

"You have no idea, yet." Chandler purred, reawakening Lettie's desire. She flipped Lettie over, straddling her. "But it's almost lunch and Daphne might be looking for you."

But she didn't seem like she wanted Lettie to leave. She was toying with her, grinding her ass against her, though without enough conviction to make it count.

Lettie glanced at the clock. It was almost eleven. And she wanted to stay, but Chandler was right. Right, but so topless. And Lettie didn't know what it would be like once she left the apartment, once real life was upon them again. "What are you doing today?"

"Meeting with the contractor. Hopefully fucking you some more." She leaned down and kissed Lettie's nose. "Paying a hefty chunk of money to get out of my old apartment's lease early?"

"Really?" Lettie tried not to sound too eager.

Chandler shrugged. "This one's free. You got out of yours, right?"

"Yeah. With a hefty chunk of change." Lettie glanced back at the clock. The sun was beaming in through the window and she had yet to think of a lie to tell Daphne. Did she even need one? She wasn't in the habit of telling her best friend lies. "I have a meeting with Pepper in an hour. I should go."

Chandler moved off her. "Is this…just a one-time thing, or…"

Lettie was surprised to hear the uncertainty in Chandler's voice. "Not if you don't want it to be." But she knew that wasn't a promise. That wasn't Chandler saying she was going to stay. That was the question she wasn't ready to ask.

The truth was, as much as Lettie planned to continue this, as much as she didn't think she had the willpower to stop, she couldn't imagine a future that ended well. And she had the Lodge to think of, that was the future she should be focusing on.

But goddamnit, Lettie was so tired of making the right choices, of always being responsible, of boxing up all the parts of her that might make others uncomfortable. She wanted to hold on to the conviction to make mistakes that had felt so all-encompassing the night before.

And Chandler was the bad choice Lettie had never been able to not make.

"Good," Chandler said. "Because you drive me wild, Lettie Katz. You always have."

"I'll see you later, okay." Lettie stood up and downed a mouthful of coffee.

"It's a date." Chandler smiled.

-CHAPTER TWELVE-

FOR A FEW moments, Lettie had hope that the apartment was empty. She needed time to think of the best way to explain to Daphne. But she had no such luck. Daphne burst out of her room, still pulling her shirt over her head.

"What. The. Fuck."

There were empty soda cans on the coffee table and Lettie reached for them, just for something to do, but Daphne tapped her foot on the floor and moved closer.

"Let me explain," Lettie started.

"Oh, no need to explain. I ran into your brother last night. And then you didn't come home, so I'm no mathematician but I think I can put two and two together."

"Okay, chill out," Lettie said, plopping down onto the couch, but she had no illusions that Daphne would. She had never chilled out a moment in her life.

"She just came back, Lettie. You own the Lodge together and she can't sell for six months. Hmm, I wonder why she'd want to get closer to you—"

"I know you're not insinuating she's sleeping with me so she can renege on the contract. Because that would be such a shitty thing to say."

"Okay? Am I supposed to only tell you nice things? Oh, Lettie, it's so good you're sleeping with the one person to ever get under your skin. I hope she rails you while you pick out paint colors because this could never, ever go wrong." Daphne sat on the coffee table and pushed her blonde hair over her shoulder before crossing her arms.

"You're being such an asshole."

"She's literally a snake, Lettie. You can't trust her."

"And you're a banshee! Should I sleep with earplugs, so you don't murder me?"

Daphne stood back up, so violently the coffee table slid back. Then she paced the length of the room so many times Lettie almost thought she wasn't going to speak again, but finally she stopped moving. "Lettie, I love you. I really do. And I want you to be happy."

"I know that." Lettie curled her feet underneath her on the couch.

"Are you just horny? Do you need to get laid? There's, like, a surprisingly large number of queer women in this town. I can get you laid."

"Daphne…"

"Okay. Okay." She threw her hands up. "Fine. I just want you to be happy. But I'm not above an 'I told you so.' Not even a little bit."

"I know that too."

Daphne crossed the room and sat beside Lettie on the old floral couch. "Does this mean I have to be nice to her?"

"You're not nice to anyone, sweetheart. I wouldn't expect you to start now."

"It's not my fault. People are just terrible." She put her head on Lettie's shoulder but quickly sat up straight again, wrinkling her nose. "You smell like her. It's gross. You've got meetings all day. You should go take a shower."

When Lettie finally made her way to the front desk, her brother was there, obviously flirting with Pepper who looked amused, but entirely uninterested. If he wasn't careful, Margery was going to have his head mounted on her wall.

"Lorne, get a job."

"I did, I was just meeting with your contractor. I'm going to do some of the woodworking on the old cabins." He grinned. "Pepper is so excited to see more of me."

"Oh, yeah. Delighted." She pulled a folder from underneath the desk. "So, the Lodge is half full starting at the end of March and the summer is basically completely full. Now, I ran the numbers you suggested for the cabins, and like you said it is much higher than the single rooms, but they have more bedrooms, so when I compare it to the prices elsewhere, I think we're right on target. And if we can fill those like we are with the rest of the Lodge, the renovations should pay for themselves. Now I had an idea regarding your lovely brother, and perhaps even Oak who has been hanging around more lately."

Lettie tried to look calm, but her heart was racing. She was doing this. Really doing it. And, best of all, it seemed to be working. She'd tried to talk Hattie and Everly into renovating the cabins for years, but they'd never agreed. Lettie had been sure there was money in it.

Maybe she wasn't making totally bad decisions, maybe there was some middle ground where she belonged, somewhere between reckless and straight laced. "Okay, let's hear the idea."

"Tours. We'd only charge a small fee, but I think the groups would be large enough to still pay them a salary. They could show off Siren Island and the town as well. Plus, I think it would pull in people from other local motels and let them see the Lodge. They'll go home and lament their choice of lodging, drumming up business for us when they complain to their friends and family. We could even have a buyer's remorse discount for future stays that we offer at the end of the tours."

"She's smart." Lorne reached across the desk and into the dish of lollipops Pepper kept on the counter, then popped one into his mouth.

"She's the best." Lettie agreed. "That's a great idea, Pepper."

The front door opened, and a family of guests came in. Lettie smiled and greeted them, then watched them head to the dining room with envy. Her stomach grumbled in agreement.

"And I ran into Amelia last night. She said she wants to work with us," Pepper said. "I'm not sure what the two of you have planned, but her festival idea is good. The bar is close enough to walk to, we could get Hershel or the Glass Fox to help cater it, or even bring in food trucks from other towns. We'd have music and vendors, and we could do it out by the lake. You own that land, but we aren't using it for anything. I was thinking early summer or late spring, before it gets too hot."

Lettie grinned. "Absolutely. Do you have time to do a write up for me? Just so I can show Chandler. Then we can make something official to send out, see who would want to be involved."

"Yeah. There are barely any customers. I can probably get it done by tomorrow."

Lettie grinned. She'd been the one to hire Pepper, back when they were both barely out of high school. Now she didn't know how the Lodge had ever run without her. "Excellent. I'm going to grab some food from the diner, but I can stop by after and help with anything you need. Plus, I wanted to peek in on Chandler's meeting with the contractor." Lettie finished up with Pepper and left, dreaming of the Reuben she was going to get.

But she didn't make it off the porch before Lorne was at her side. She tried to ignore him, shielding her eyes from the midday sun, but he kept pace with her, grinning like an idiot, the lollipop jutting out of his mouth.

"Hey sis. How was your boat ride?" He wiggled his eyebrows. "Feeling stiff this morning? Spent the night as stone?"

"I don't know how anyone finds you charming, you dense asshole." But she had to fight to keep the smile off her lips. Still, this wasn't something she was about to discuss with her brother, of all people. "Does Margery know you're flirting with Pepper?"

She tried to walk faster than her brother and turned a corner onto a nearly empty street. The sun might be out, but it wasn't doing much good, the temperature grew colder by the day.

Her brother followed her onto the sidewalk, putting a hand over his heart. "You wound me, Lettie. I only want to make sure my dearest, darling sister is happy. I came to the Lodge only for you, never to flirt."

"I'm going to hit you." She quickened her pace, but he had six inches on her and kept up easily.

He knocked his shoulder against hers. "Does the mayor know about the two of you? Should we put the fire department on high alert?" He ducked when she swung at him. "Come on, Lettie. I let you borrow my boat. Doesn't that earn me a little gossip? Nothing ever happens here."

"Yes," she said, "Happy?"

"Absolutely. Gestin knew it! Gran would be so happy." He wrapped his arm around her shoulder. "And I think you're right. I should go talk to Margery."

"I absolutely did not say that." She also didn't think anything she did the night before was what her grandmother had in mind when she concocted her plan with Everly. Monica might be proud though. The thought sobered her.

"You said something like that. It was the spirit of it. See ya later, sis."

She watched as he left, then leaned against the wall outside a coffee shop. She had things she should do, and she was still starving, but somewhere back at the Lodge was Chandler. She pulled out her phone.

Do you want something to eat? I'm going to Hershel's. The grease helps to soak up the booze.

She shoved her phone back into her pocket and continued her walk, holding up her hand to watch sparks of magic dance along her fingertips.

When she got to the diner, Hershel was there, grinning under his bushy gray beard. She greeted him and ordered a sandwich.

"Coming right up."

"Thanks." Her phone dinged with a message.

I ate already, but I've still got an appetite ;) The contractor is chatty so it may be a while. Meet me here when you're done?

Heat shot through Lettie and, inexplicably, she thought of Daphne who had been telling her she needed to get laid for months. Maybe she had been right.

She was too old to be feeling this way—like a horny teenager ready to dive in headfirst—but she hadn't yet forgotten the conclusion she had come to before. A lifetime of careful planning and double thinking every choice hadn't gotten her very far.

She raked her hands through her hair, lost in thought. Could this really end in anything but heartbreak? Did she care? She'd kept her heart perfectly safe all these years, maybe it needed a crack or two. Certainly, the memory of Chandler calling her a good girl was making all of her thoughts irrational, and the gorgon was in town either way. As long as she kept her heart in check and didn't forget this was a fling with a six month expiration date, she'd be okay.

"Lettie, are you alright? You look a little pale." Herschel returned from the back and pushed a paper bag across the counter.

"Oh, yeah. Of course. Just stressed dealing with all the Stone and Sorcery stuff." She smiled, wrapping her fingers around the bag. The smell of sauerkraut and corned beef made her mouth water.

"Oh, honey. You're going to do great. You've got the same fire as Hattie had." The old man's kindness shone through his wrinkled features. There was a reason that his diner was always full. He reached across the counter and covered her hand with his. "You've always got a warm meal and a friend here, as long as you don't bring that brother of yours." He winked.

"Now, come on. I'm sure Lorne would have starved years ago without you."

"Maybe I'm too nice. Or maybe I'm scared of you witches. It's not easy being a human in this town."

Try being a witch with an ex back in town. "Now, Herschel. What have witches ever done to you?"

"I was young once, Lettie Katz, and you don't want to hear my stories involving witches. Now go on, before that sandwich gets soggy. It's better fresh."

She lifted the bag in a mock salute. As she walked out into the watery winter sunlight, her now familiar mantra played through her head. *Get it together, Lettie Katz.*

At least, whatever happened, she was going to be the best damn inn owner the south had ever seen. Watch out Conrad Hilton. There was a new name in town. She chuckled to herself, and her phone dinged again in her pocket.

I can't focus on a word this contractor is saying. I want to bury myself in you.

Lettie flushed, trying to think of something to text back. This was not her strong suit. Lettie did romance, bringing girls flowers and holding their hand. But this was hot, sweltering, totally out of her comfort zone.

And she liked it.

She really, really liked it.

She stopped at her apartment only long enough to cram her sandwich into her mouth, still unable to think of any return texts to send. She brushed her hair, and switched out her shirt to something lower cut, then looked herself over in the mirror.

She looked good. Her cheeks were flushed and there was something else, something she couldn't name but that she liked. Not quite a whole new Lettie, but a freer one, one who no longer felt the crushing weight of self-imposed expectations she could never live up to.

Most importantly, she looked hot. She rushed outside, towards the cabins, where the buzz of saws covered the sounds of the lake. Chandler was standing across from the contractor in a peacoat, her dark hair pulled into a ponytail, one hand on her hip.

Lettie slowed her pace and tugged her shirt down a little lower, taking a moment to appreciate the scene, the sunlight catching in Chandler's curls, the scent of wood in the air, and the property she owned spread out before her.

Chandler spotted her, and her mouth curved into a sly smile. She said something Lettie couldn't hear to the contractor and broke away, heading across the grass.

Before Lettie could say anything, Chandler grabbed her by the wrist and pulled her behind a cabin. In record speed, Chandler had her pushed against the side of the building, her mouth on Lettie's, her hands under her shirt.

She broke away as quickly as she had started, her eyes wide and full of mischief. She grinned, motioning to the air around Lettie, where vibrant green magic sparkled. "Well, look at that, you little witch."

"What have you done to me?" Lettie whispered, basking in the warmth that spread through her. All the way down to her core.

"Oh, I'm going to do all kinds of things to you." She ran her thumb over Lettie's lower lip. "We should work though."

"I know." But Lettie needed a minute to catch her breath, sure the contractor would hear her pulse racing. And less sure with each passing minute, each clandestine touch, of what she was doing.

"You aren't going to believe this, but he thinks he could fit a third bedroom in some of the cabins. We could charge even more."

"Yeah? It might leave money to redo some geriatric apartments, right?" Lettie shoved her hands into her pockets to keep from reaching for Chandler.

"I really like the way you think, Katz."

-CHAPTER THIRTEEN-

THE PAST THREE days had been spent almost entirely with the contractor. Though he was talented, and his team was excellent, Lettie was still Lettie, and she had trouble letting go, especially when so many important decisions were being made. So, she had stayed out in the cold, overseeing the progress, until she was sure everyone else understood her vision for the cabins and the future of the Lodge.

And as much as she'd wanted to slip back into Chandler's bed—and she had managed it the night before—she'd been absolutely exhausted.

And now this?

"Please, Lettie." Daphne pouted. "Come to the Sisters with me. Come on. Don't make me go alone."

An evening listening to a drunk Daphne list all the things wrong with Chandler wasn't what she had in mind. She had been planning on a warm bath and blissful silence. "I was—"

"*Fine.* You know what? I'm a whole new banshee." Daphne marched dramatically across the living room and flung the door open. Lettie cringed at the sound of her knocking on Chandler's door.

"Yeah?" Chandler's voice was full of suspicion.

"You can't just fuck her. You've got to take her out too," Daphne said.

Lettie was going to sink right into the floorboards, but before she could figure out how to shed her body and disappear, Chandler came across the hall, followed closely by Daphne.

"You want to go to a bar tonight?" she asked. Her arms were crossed over her chest, and she cut her eyes at Daphne.

"I didn't necessarily say that."

"But do you?"

Did she? The bath did sound nice, but she'd been answering emails, picking paint colors, and sourcing wood samples all day. Maybe a little fun wouldn't hurt. "Yeah, a little."

Chandler chewed her bottom lip. "Okay. We've still got that meeting tomorrow morning though."

"You can leave early. I'm not picky." Daphne was grinning like a possum.

"Okay." Chandler dropped her arms to her sides. "See you later, Letts. Daphne, always a…pleasure."

"Mmhmm. I bet." Daphne pulled the door shut behind her. "See you just gotta ask."

"I wasn't planning on asking. I think I said I didn't want to go." She began to go to her bedroom then stopped. She was always letting stuff go, but she wasn't a doormat. "Actually, you know what, Daphne? That was fucked up. You can't do shit like that. Whatever is going on between me and Chandler is *our* business. I told you because you're supposed to be my best friend. Everything isn't a game."

Daphne's face fell. "Lettie, I just thought—"

"Did you? Did you think at all beyond the tip of your nose? Did you care for one moment how I might feel, or were you just worried about what might be funny? I let you live here for free; I've supported you in *everything* my whole life. She's right across the fucking hall. If I had wanted to ask her to go to the bar, I would have asked her myself."

"Okay. You're right. I'm sorry. You're absolutely right. I wasn't thinking about it like that, I was thinking how you asked me to back off, give her a chance. I thought a little booze might facilitate that, but I should have listened to you. I'll do better." Daphne took a step towards Lettie, approaching her like she was a caged animal. "I'm really sorry. I know I'm an asshole, but I try to keep that away from you."

The fight left Lettie. She motioned Daphne closer and hugged her. "You are an asshole, but I forgive you," she said as she pulled away.

"I'll behave, I promise." Daphne sighed as she moved away from Lettie and curled into the window seat. Bathed in the bright winter sun, her white hair shone like glass.

The image was striking. She could be a painting, or a picture they put in a brochure. The thought filled Lettie with joy. The Lodge was hers, the beautiful, history filled building where the two strongest women she knew had lived their lives and filled the halls with laughter and love. Though the burden of everything in front of her was still heavy, remembering her Gran made it a little lighter. This wasn't just a job, it was her legacy, something she could be proud of.

And as annoying as Daphne could be, Lettie was glad to have her around.

She ran her fingers over the details in the woodworking around the window, tiny flowers, too small to see unless you were close. There were little imperfections—on the windowsill, the wall, the door jambs. Places where someone had knocked into them, where children's toys had flown and scratched the wood. Her Gran had called those spots proof of life. What marks would Lettie leave?

She slid into the seat beside Daphne. "So, what about you? When are you going to settle down?"

"I don't know, thirty, forty years?" She leaned across Lettie, propping the window open. "My answer is the same as it always is; I'm not interested."

Lettie knew she should drop it. She hadn't appreciated Daphne butting in her business earlier, but that was exactly the reason she kept going. Sometimes Daphne just seemed so frustrated, frustrated and lonely. She'd never had a relationship, never been in love. They'd been friends since they were kids, which was how Lettie knew she was the only person Daphne had ever truly opened up to. And despite her flaws, Lettie thought Daphne deserved to be loved. "You're not interested in anyone? Amelia? What about Lorne? You've been flirting with him since we were kids."

"You want me to date Lorne?" Daphne raised her eyebrows.

"Well, no, obviously I don't. But if you wanted to, I wouldn't want you not to on account of me."

Daphne barked with laughter, making Lettie's ears ring. "I don't want to date Lorne. And that is something you're going to want to take at face value."

And she certainly would. She had her suspicions about what went on between Daphne and her brother, but she'd never pried, and she didn't intend to start, at least not any further than a light teasing. "And Amelia?"

"Amelia is…we're friends. You know that. You're being weird." The wind blew in through the window, picking up strands of Daphne's hair. "This is revenge, isn't it?"

Lettie shrugged. "Maybe a little. It's mild though, don't you think?" She pulled her phone out of her pocket and tapped her fingers on the black screen. "If I wanted to take a page out of your book, I could call Amelia."

"Do. Not." Daphne's eyes widened. "I'll scream."

"You will not." Lettie jumped off the window seat and walked backwards. She shook her phone, enjoying terrorizing Daphne. "What to say? Hey Amelia, Daphne thinks we have to go to your bar every other night, and I think I know why. I think it's the allure of auburn hair and—"

Daphne leapt from the seat, scrambling towards Lettie. "Stop. You wouldn't. You're just a nuisance."

Lettie put her phone back in her pocket. "I'm just looking out for you. I want you to be happy."

"A little sex and you think you've got it all figured out," Daphne teased. "And it's the only bar in town. That doesn't mean I want to fuck the owner. Jesus, Lettie. Can't two women just be friends?"

Lettie rolled her eyes, headed for the kitchen, and pulled the kettle out of a cabinet. "Seriously though, you'll be chill tonight? With Chandler?"

"I will," Daphne said, following her. "I have said all I have to say. I'll be nothing but pleasant."

Somehow Lettie still had her doubts. She filled the kettle with water and put it on the stove. "Daph, am I being an idiot?"

"An idiot? No. You've never been an idiot. You're just uptight and now you've got more responsibility than you're used to. It's normal to need an outlet for that. And she's cute. Just…never mind."

"No. Say it." Lettie reached for her favorite mug and wrapped her fingers around it.

"Has she said she's going to stay?"

"No. And I'm too chickenshit to ask again." She wished the tea was ready, that the cup in her hands was warm and comforting.

Daphne walked closer and grabbed her own cup, pressing herself into Lettie's space. "Then don't put your whole heart in. Not yet. Let it be what it is."

None of that was what Lettie wanted to hear, but she nodded. *Let it be what it is.* And right now, it was fun. She was having a great time. Chandler was hot and funny and great in bed. And Lettie was no stranger to short-lived relationships. She nodded again.

The advice was good. Wasn't that all she had wanted? To let loose, to stop being, as Daphne put it, uptight. "Am I really that tightly wound?"

"Yeah, but, like, in a very endearing way."

"I don't think that's a thing."

Daphne scoffed. "Don't tell me how I feel." She reached above Lettie and grabbed the tea bags. "Let me do your make-up tonight."

"You need more friends, you know that? More people to bother." Lettie plucked a bag of green tea from the container. "And yes, obviously. I'm terrible at it."

-CHAPTER FOURTEEN-

WHAT WAS THE protocol for dating someone who lived across the hall from you? Lettie wasn't sure. Did she knock on Chandler's door? Wait for Chandler to knock on hers? Meet her in the lobby? At the bar?

Okay, maybe she *was* a little uptight. The realization didn't answer any of her questions. A knock on the front door made her heart skip a beat.

But when she made it to the living room, it was only her brother standing there. "I was working on the cabins, and Daphne said y'all were going out."

"Does it get weird? You know, drinking where you work?"

"It's a small town. And I'm cutting back on shifts. I like the carpentry." Lorne grinned, his shaggy blonde hair falling into his eyes. "I thought I would walk you ladies over. I was going in that direction, anyway."

Lorne seemed happy, there was a sparkle in his eyes Lettie rarely saw. Maybe working with the contractor and being part of the Lodge again would do him some good, give him a purpose. He'd learned to work with wood from their grandfather, and he'd always excelled at it. He used to whittle Lettie gifts when they were kids. She still had a box of tiny wooden animals tucked away under her bed.

"You can walk me." Daphne dramatically fluttered her lashes at him. "Since your sister thinks we're in love."

Lorne's cheeks turned red. "What?"

"I didn't say that," Lettie said and Daphne burst into laughter.

"Come on, Lorne." Daphne looped her arm through his and he lowered his head, whispering something.

No, she *really* didn't want to know what went on between the two of them. Lorne and Daphne left together, giggling over whatever Lorne had whispered.

Leaving Lettie alone in her apartment, dressed up and unsure. This was dumb; just standing there, waiting, when she knew Chandler was across the hallway.

She went across the hall, but before she could lift her hand Chandler's door swung open. She froze at the sight of Lettie. She was wearing a leather jacket over a white t-shirt tucked into dark green jeans. Lettie's eyes couldn't help but follow the fabric, rounded over the curves of her breasts and smooth across her abdomen.

"Hey."

"Hey." Chandler smiled, tucking a strand of hair behind her ear. "You look really nice."

"Thanks, so do you. I'm sorry about Daphne."

"No big deal. That's not even in the top ten worst interactions I've had with her. In fact, it might be one of the best. Hope you don't mind but I think Oak is going to come by. I figured I could use the backup."

"Oh, that's fine." Lettie had always liked Oak. The shifter had moved to Lilac Lake when they were both in elementary school and they had passed summer afternoons by riding bikes around the lake together. Their friendship had petered out as they grew older, but Lettie had always kept a soft spot for them.

"They might be, um…They're happy I'm back. Thrilled, really. They did not like Gwen when they visited me last year."

Gwen. The mysterious human woman. Or at least mysterious to Lettie who had plenty of questions she had no right to ask.

"So, you ready to go?" Chandler asked.

Lettie pushed her questions down. "I'm ready if you are."

Outside the Stone and Sorcery Lodge, Chandler wrapped her arm around Lettie. "You better leave with me tonight."

"Play your cards right," Lettie teased, but she leaned into the embrace.

"Oh, yeah. Thinking of testing out your options?" Chandler stopped walking, glanced back at the Lodge, then kissed Lettie roughly on the mouth before moving her lips to Lettie's ear. "Feel free to do what you want. But I already know the things you like."

Goosebumps broke out over Lettie's skin, her whole body tight and hot. "Think you've got me all figured out?"

"Oh, not nearly. But I'm beginning to get the idea." Chandler raised an eyebrow.

They continued to make their way across town and Lettie tried her best not to enjoy the weight of Chandler's arm around her. Not to notice the way their bodies fit together perfectly. She tried to just enjoy the moment, not wonder at the future, but every time they were together it grew more difficult.

Music came from the open door of The Three Sisters and they both stopped walking. Lettie could see people she knew through the window; Amelia cleaning the bar, Margery with her head thrown back laughing, her blonde hair neatly curled.

This was it. The whole town was going to see them. And there was nothing better to do in a tiny town than gossip. She had no doubt they'd both be getting visits from their mothers soon.

"We don't have to…" Lettie said.

"If you aren't ready…" Chandler cleared her throat.

Guilt pooled in Lettie's core. "I'm not embarrassed or anything. It's just that we own a business together, and in any other place we could just go to a bar, but here, once we go in, that's it. Everyone knows and I don't—we haven't—"

"Just as friends then, officially. No touching?" Chandler nudged Lettie's hip, a playfulness to her voice. "Might be fun."

Lettie smiled. "We'd have to get our friends to shut up though."

"*Your* friends. I have one friend and they won't mind. So, what do you say, Lettie? Secret lovers for a night?" Chandler dropped her arm from Lettie's waist and put out her hand.

Lettie shook it, though she already wanted Chandler's arm back around her. "A little ruse. To keep our sanity."

Together they entered the bar, a respectable distance between them. The music pounded, and the light was low, leaving shadows in the corners. There would be no performance by the sisters tonight, but the bar still crawled with patrons, many of whom Lettie recognized.

"I'll be right back." Chandler headed towards the bar, where Oak was on a barstool talking to Amelia.

Lettie spotted Daphne near the pool tables and her friend threw her arms up, rushing forward to wrap Lettie in a hug that smelled like tequila.

"Okay, quick note. Chandler and I aren't ready to tell everyone yet. We want the town focused on the renovations, not us. So, keep your mouth shut? Please?"

"Okay." Daphne nodded and pretended to zip up her lips and tuck an invisible key in her pocket. "Come dance."

"I'm going to get a drink first." Lettie headed for Oak and Chandler at the bar. She couldn't hear what Chandler was saying but Oak was nodding.

"Hey!" They grinned when she got closer. "It's good to see you. I've got her first one, Amelia." Oak winked at Lettie.

"Whiskey sour. Thanks." Lettie wasn't sure what she was supposed to do, tucked between two barstools and pretending she didn't want to make out with the woman next to her. "Hey, Chandler. Good to see you."

"You too." Chandler was nearly dismissive, but she slid into the seat next to Lettie. "What brings you out…partner?"

"You sound like a cowboy." Amelia slid the whiskey sour across the bar.

"You should see me ride a horse." Chandler wrapped her fingers around her glass and brought it to her smirking lips.

"Mmm, pass." Amelia wiped up a wet spot on the bar.

"Come on, dance with me." Daphne appeared on Lettie's other side. "Wait. First, two shots, please." She held up two fingers at Amelia.

Going home early seemed further and further away with each drink her friends bought her, but Lettie grabbed the shot glass, clinked it against Daphne's, and downed it with a grimace.

The tequila burned her throat and warmed her belly. She followed it with a long drink of her whiskey sour—a horrible combination—then Daphne dragged her onto the mostly deserted dance floor.

"Margery! Oak!" She yelled across the bar, her voice cutting through the din of the crowd and turning heads. Oak pulled Chandler with them, and Margery grabbed Lorne.

Lettie gave in to the music, swaying her body to the beat as Daphne laughed, twirling around the edges of the dance floor.

"You seem happy, girl," Margery said, moving away from Lorne to dance in front of Lettie. "It's good to see."

"It's good to feel." Lettie took another drink from the tray Amelia brought over and danced towards Daphne. She tried not to look at Chandler, the way her body moved, the sway of her hips or the curve of her ass. Or those long fingers, wrapped around her drink. Fingers that…Good grief, she really needed a distraction.

She should not have let Daphne talk her into this. Maybe she should go home. She continued towards Daphne to let her know she was leaving.

But Oak got there before she did. They whispered something to Daphne, and she smiled, then the two of them were gone, heading towards the bar.

And Margery was back to dancing with Lorne.

Leaving Chandler and Lettie on the dance floor beside each other. And she really did look good, the tight jeans accentuating her delicious curves, and her face flushed from dancing. Lettie moved closer and Chandler did the same.

"I want to feel you," Lettie whispered.

Chandler's eyes were like shards of stone beneath a stormy sea; verdant waves crashing on the shore and waiting to pull Lettie under. "Come." She stepped back and turned, heading for the bathroom.

Lettie glanced at the bar, where Daphne, Amelia and Oak were doing shots.

This was not what she did. Lettie did not hook up in bar bathrooms. Yet she kept walking, moving toward the dim hallway. She pushed open the bathroom door, and Chandler's fingers wrapped around the collar of her jacket, pulling her inside.

She blinked in the darkness and heard the lock click before Chandler turned on the lights. They flickered overhead, the fluorescents on their last leg.

Before she had time to think, Chandler's mouth was on hers, her fingers tangled in Lettie's hair, pushing her against the sink.

Lettie gripped Chandler's hips, and she lifted Lettie onto the damp counter. With expert ease, she pulled Lettie's tights down and pressed her lips to her throat.

Lettie braced her hands on the counter, and wrapped her legs around Chandler, pulling her closer. "Just friendly, right?"

"Gal pals." Chandlers ran her tongue down the length of Lettie's neck and moved her hands to her thighs, spreading them apart. "Is this okay?" She ran a finger over the front of Lettie's panties.

"Yes." The words came out breathless, and Lettie wanted more, more friction, more hands on her skin. *Just more.* Every inch she could get. She reached for Chandler, but the gorgon slapped her hand away.

"And this?" Chandler dropped to her knees, the noise echoing through the bathroom. She ran her tongue over the fabric of Lettie's underwear, then hooked her thumbs on either side, yanking down.

"Yes." Lettie contorted herself, desperate to rid herself of her panties. She pulled them from her ankles and threw them in a pile with her leggings.

"You looked so delicious." Chandler's breath was hot against her wet clit. She gripped Lettie by the ass, pulling her closer. Slowly, she kissed up her thigh and then closer, right beside the spot where Lettie's body ached so desperately for Chandler.

Lettie rocked her hips, overcome with the need for more friction. Chandler chuckled, and for a moment Lettie thought she wouldn't comply and groaned with disappointment.

Instead, Chandler buried her face in Lettie's sex, and she had to bite her lip to keep from yelling out so loudly the entire bar would hear.

Chandler held her tight, running tight, fast circles over Lettie's clit, bringing her to the edge faster than anyone ever had before.

The gorgon dug her fingers into Lettie's thigh with one hand, holding tight and slipped two fingers inside Lettie with the other. Lettie's back arched and she knocked her head into the paper towel dispenser, but she barely noticed, writhing her body against Chandler.

Her whole body felt tight, pulled to a single point as Chandler ran her tongue against Lettie's center, again and again. And then the point exploded, and Lettie worried she would break the sink as her body shook with release.

Chandler slowed as she pulled her fingers from Lettie. She moved lower, tasting Lettie's entrance before returning her mouth to Lettie's thighs and kissing her gently where her nails had left marks.

Lettie had never come so fast in her life. She'd forgotten where she was, who she was, her only thoughts were for the woman who still knelt between her thighs on the grimy bathroom floor, looking up at her with sea storm eyes.

When Chandler finally stood, she kissed Lettie, cupping her breasts, and Lettie fumbled with the button of Chandler's jeans before sliding her hand down between the layers of fabric.

Chandler was soaking wet, and she shuddered at Lettie's touch. There was no time for seduction. Soon someone would come looking for them.

Lettie pressed two fingers against her clit, and Chandler's fingernails dug into the skin of Lettie's back. With Chandler's hands on her, Lettie's whole body felt light, and she wondered if she could bring Chandler to orgasm as quickly as the gorgon had done for her.

If Chandler's groans against the skin of her neck was any indication, it would not be a difficult task. Lettie lowered her feet to the floor and drove Chandler across the tiles until she was pressed against the wall of the bathroom.

She ripped Chandler's pants down, just as Chandler had done to Lettie, and knelt between her thighs. Lettie looked up to find Chandler staring at her, her eyes wide, pupils blown out. "Is this what you want from me? If we weren't in this bathroom? What dirty deeds?"

Before Chandler could answer, Lettie pressed her mouth to Chandler's core, flicking her tongue against her clit. She was so wet, delicious and ready. Lettie licked the length of her, and Chandler's hand curled into her hair, her nails rough against Lettie's scalp.

"This is good, but not this," Chandler said. "I like this, but I like it better when I make you scream." Her voice was low, and she moaned between words. "I like the way you look when you come."

Lettie pressed her own thighs together as she kept moving her tongue over Chandler.

"Touch yourself." Chandler demanded, pulling at Lettie's hair until she gazed up at her. "Touch yourself while you taste me."

Lettie gulped, but she moved her fingers between her thighs, brushing them hesitantly against her throbbing clit, as she moved her mouth back to Chandler.

The gorgon held her head tight as she ground herself against Lettie, and Lettie pushed her fingers in tight circles against her own sex, the hard tiles digging into her bare knees.

As her own pleasure increased, Chandler moved more frantically against her, letting out little noises that filled the bathroom. With a shudder Chandler came on Lettie's lips, and it only took two more swipes of her fingers before she came too, throwing her head back, and trying not to yell, even if it was what Chandler wanted.

The gorgon urged her up and captured her mouth in a kiss that tasted like both of them. "God, Lettie."

Someone pounded on the bathroom door, and Lettie squealed.

"Are you done? Some of us have to pee!" Daphne yelled.

"I don't think anyone noticed." Chandler winked.

-CHAPTER FIFTEEN-

HAD THAT JUST happened?

Lettie headed straight for the bar, not daring to turn around and look for Chandler behind her, though she could feel the other woman's presence, the cool, dark touch of her magic. And she could feel her own, the bright, vibrant ball of it dancing around in her stomach.

Or maybe that was nerves. Or both. Either way Lettie needed a drink. And a cold shower. Amelia offered her a shot and she, and downed it, but all it did was add to the heat burning through her.

Bathroom hookups and secret lovers were something other girls did. Fun girls. Girls who partied on weekdays and couldn't count everyone they'd slept with on their fingers. Girls who weren't afraid to take what they wanted and never felt sorry about it. Now Lettie was that kind of girl. And she kind of loved it.

She'd been good all her life. Sensible. Responsible. Was that still her? Was all her recent behavior some sort of aberration? A one-third life crisis? Was that a thing?

Lettie twirled her finger above the top of her beer, and the booze danced, amber drops of liquid rising and twisting before reuniting with the others.

"Look at that." Amelia smiled. "It's good to get it out. That's why I sing. I can never let my power fully out, I'd never do that to anyone, but being on stage is like letting the steam out of a pressure pot. It helps me to not explode. We've all worried about you."

"Who is all?" Lettie glanced across the bar, where her brother was throwing darts while Margery lounged on one of the tattered couches.

"Yeah. That's mostly all. But he does worry about you. In his own way. So…" Amelia cut her eyes across the bar. "You and Chandler?"

"What?" Lettie rested her chin on her hand. "Oh, us running the Lodge?"

Amelia threw her head back laughing. "You're a bad fucking liar, Lettie Katz. But if it's like that, then my lips are sealed. I know a few things about secret lovers."

"Is it true then?" Lettie nearly jumped across the bar. "You and Daphne?"

"What?" Amelia's confusion was genuine. Lettie could feel her cheeks heat, embarrassment coursing through her. "Who told you I was sleeping with Daphne?"

"No one." Lettie downed her drink. "Seriously. I just had this theory. Daphne said I was being an idiot, and—I'm going to shut up now."

Tapping her fingers on the bar, Amelia squinted, and this time Lettie didn't need to follow her line of sight to know what she was looking at. "The dating pool in this town is more like a puddle, or a spilled cup of water."

"Hence the hanky-panky with my ex who I should be building a business relationship with."

"Don't ever say hanky-panky again," Amelia teased. "Though I would keep it quiet because your mothers are really something, and if they hear, whew." She grimaced and shook her head. "The cabins look great, by the way. I'm really looking forward to that festival."

"We should get lunch sometime. Really plan it out. I know you have an eye for those things." She'd only been to Amelia's house a couple of times, but it was fantastic, over-decorated in the best way, like a museum of curiosities and jewel toned paints. And she'd seen her throw small events in the bar and out on town square. The woman could really do the most with any theme.

"That would be great, Lettie. Look at us. Town businesswomen. Who would have guessed we'd end up here back when we used to get drunk in the woods."

Chandler slid into the seat beside Lettie and the wood wavered in front of her—stone and back. Her cheeks were still flushed. "Sorry to eavesdrop, but do you remember your senior prom?"

"Who could forget the way Principal Mansfield screamed when she touched that snake." Amelia laughed, but it fell from her face when she went to pour Chandler a drink and found the shot glass stone. "You okay?"

Chandler glanced down. "Oh. Just feeling a little…emotional. Sorry." She tapped her finger on the glass and it changed back. "I should get going. I'll see you later, Letts."

"Yeah, see ya." Lettie almost bent over, almost kissed her in the bar. Instead, she dug her nails into the barstool and watched Chandler leave.

"Did something…" Amelia cleared her throat. "She seemed tense."

"Yeah," Lettie stared at the still swinging door Chandler had disappeared behind, trying to puzzle out what had happened to bother her and coming up short. Was it the sex? Was it Lettie? But no matter how she put the pieces together the picture didn't get clearer.

"Hey, perk up," Amelia said. "She's always been capricious."

"Yeah, sure." Lettie turned back to the bar and put a smile on her face. If she spent all her time trying to figure out Chandler, she'd never get anything done. Eventually the gorgon would tell her…or she wouldn't.

Lettie stood up, stretched her hands above her head, and headed back towards the dance floor to rejoin her friends.

There were days that Lettie was glad to live in the south, and most of those days happened during the warm respites occasionally offered by winter, when the sun would shine warmer than it had in weeks and spring would suddenly seem just around the corner.

Daphne had thrown open every window, though the temperature hovered in the mid-sixties. "I love this place." She spread her arms and spun in a circle. "Maybe once Chandler runs off, I can take her apartment and we'll each have our own."

Lettie froze, a piece of toast halfway to her mouth.

"Oh, Jesus." Daphne stopped spinning. "Foot meet mouth. I am so sorry."

"It's fine." Lettie could still feel the cold tile of the bathroom beneath her knees. The pinch of Chandler's nails digging into her skin. "Here for a good time, not for a long time."

"I think that's about dying, Letts." Daphne swiped half a piece of toast and took a bite.

"If the simile fits…" She stood up, pushing her plate towards Daphne. "I'm going to run to the store. We're out of…well, most things. I'll be back in like an hour. I've got a meeting. Need anything?"

Daphne shook her head. "Nah. I'll be gone by the time you get back. I've got class. I'll be home later if you want to get dinner."

"Sure." Lettie grabbed a sweater and pulled it on. "I'll see you later. Good luck in class."

Outside winter battled against the heat of the sun. In patches of light, it was warm, but the shade was cool, so Lettie tried to stay in the sun as she walked down Main Street.

Bread. Coffee. Creamer. Pizza rolls. She repeated the list in her head, though it was written in her phone. Maybe she would get one of those frozen coconut cream pies they kept near the popsicles to pair with a box of wine. The epitome of class.

She dragged her fingers along an azalea bush and was surprised to find a snake coiled in its leaves. The serpent lifted its head and gazed up at her.

"Oh, hello little guy." Her magic sparked at her fingertips.

The snake's tongue darted out, red and thin, to test the air. Lettie never found snakes. Robins and lizards and frogs, yes. But not snakes. Why had this one found her? Pure coincidence or something more?

There were other gorgons in town. And snakes existed outside of their pull. But she couldn't help herself. She looked around, scanning the nearby buildings for a familiar sharp face, for curly black hair like snakes of its own.

And she spotted her, sitting in a booth at Hershel's Diner. Lettie almost raised her hand to wave, but then she noticed the look on Chandler's face, pinched and stressed.

Lettie knew she should keep walking, but she moved closer to the diner and into the shade of an enormous oak. There was another woman across the booth from Chandler. Her blonde hair was cut into a short bob, and she had thick-rimmed glasses that suited her face.

The two women were arguing, and Lettie wished she could hear what they were saying. She wished she could leave. But Lettie was as rooted to the spot as the tree above her head. She watched them argue, unable to turn away.

Chandler pinched the bridge of her nose, and when she looked up, she said something that made the other woman reach for her hand across the table. For a moment they sat like that, Chandler's hand in someone else's.

Then she drew back, shaking her head, saying more words that Lettie couldn't hear. The woman stood and slung her purse across her shoulder, then bent down.

For a second, Lettie thought they were going to kiss, and she lurched forward, but their lips never met, and the woman straightened.

Before she left, she paused. One last look at Chandler, one last word, and then she was leaving, and Chandler put her head down on the table.

Lettie rushed forward but stopped short. What was she going to do? Burst into the diner? For all the fun she'd had with Chandler, the gorgon had never promised her anything, had never made any reference to a relationship. And Lettie didn't know where she stood. Even if she did, she didn't know what she would say. *"Oh hey, I saw you arguing with a stranger and watched like a pervert outside the window. Please tell me the details."*

The woman came out of the diner and to Lettie's horror she started walking right towards her. Lettie's fight or flight kicked in and she almost fled back to the safety of the Stone and Sorcery, but pride kept her from running.

The woman was taller than Lettie, and very pretty, with the air of someone used to wearing heels and being professional. Perfectly coiffed hair, a white, ironed blazer with a black blouse underneath. "I hope you can help me."

"Me?" Lettie brushed off the front of her shirt, a stupid crop top with two cats howling like wolves on the front.

"Yeah, you look local. Some kind of…I don't know. Siren? Witch? Who knows what's around here."

"Excuse me?" Lettie took a step back. "Who the hell are you?"

The woman rolled her eyes. "I'm Gwen Montgomery. I work for Northend Realty Services. One of my clients is buying a little motel around here. Can you point me in the direction of the, shit, Sword and Sorcery?"

"The Stone and Sorcery? No, the hell, I can't. You aren't buying that." Lettie's fingernails dug into her skin. She wanted to shake the woman. She wanted to cry. She glanced back at the diner to see Chandler staring at her with a horrified expression.

"Yeah, I'm hearing a lot of that suddenly. The papers are signed though. Oh, god." The woman laughed. "Are you Lettie?" She looked Lettie up and down before turning her attention back to the diner. Her eyes fluttered shut, and she took a deep breath. "You're smaller than I imagined."

The world felt upside down and the air too thin. Words fumbled through Lettie's brain, but she could barely make sense of what she was hearing.

"Well…I'm sure I can find it on my own. Nice to meet you, Lettie." The woman turned on her expensive heels and walked away.

Lettie wanted to cry, to sink down onto the pavement and have a good sob. She'd allowed herself to get lost in a fantasy, to be hopeful and dream of a future no one had promised her. And now she didn't know what to do.

Before she could give into any of her urges, Chandler was outside, her chest rising and falling with rapid breaths. "Lettie, please let me explain."

She wasn't going to cry. Whatever happened, she would not cry until she was home. "Explain what? That you've been lying right to my face? That you fucked me knowing full well *Gwen Montgomery* was going to show up and shatter my dreams? Actually, yeah, tell me the plan. You can't sell for six months, so what papers were signed?"

"Come on, let's sit down." Chandler moved towards a bench, but Lettie planted her feet. "Okay, we'll stay here. Can I just say I'm sorry and—"

"No. You can't. I don't want to hear it. Tell me the deal you made. I deserve to know."

Chandler ran her hands through her hair and a snake hissed from somewhere nearby. The air fizzled with magic making Lettie realize Chandler was right. She needed to sit down before something happened that would leave her full of another decade of regret.

She sat on the nearest bench and put her hands under her legs to keep from wrapping her arms around herself. "Your grandmother would be so ashamed."

Chandler sat, the wood underneath her turning to stone. The coils of her hair were tight and dark magic moved around her like puffs of smoke. "I know she would be. I really fucked up, Lettie. I was trying to fix it before you found out.

"Fix what?" Lettie's magic was hot, a pit of fire burning through her, urging her towards chaos. She needed to get control. For the first time in her life, she understood how witches cursed people.

"You have to understand I called Gwen the day I found out about the Lodge and the inheritance. Way before anything happened between us. I missed her, I thought I had a way in. I knew she still had a contract with my old employer. They were buying up real estate in towns like this and I took the opportunity."

"But you can't even sell for six months."

Chandler chewed her bottom lip. "Hillchamp is just some small-town lawyer. I don't think he even made any changes to what our grandmothers wrote up. The wording is vague. So, I signed a deal that doesn't go through until the six months are up."

Maybe Lettie *was* going to cry. "You were never planning to stay, were you?"

"No, it wasn't like that. I had a bad day. My grandmother was dead, I was missing my ex. I did something incredibly stupid, and I'm trying so hard to get out of it." Chandler reached for Lettie, but she moved away. Chandler dropped her hands back to her lap and stared at them. "Lettie, I won't let them have it. I promise."

"You can't promise that."

"I can. I really can. Look, if I back out, I lose a ton of money, but I *can* back out. I will, I swear, I will. But Lettie…" Chandler pivoted on the bench to look into Lettie's eyes. "Maybe you could help me."

"Help you? Why would I help you?" But Lettie's heartbeat had slowed, the desire to cry, or scream, or blow up the town square for a second time receding.

The bench underneath Chandler changed back to wood. "Because you have pity for idiots? Because, maybe, just a little, you believe that I'm very, very sorry."

"Fine." Lettie crossed her arms over her chest. "I'm not agreeing, but I'll listen."

Chandler smiled, and her entire face lit up with relief. "If I back out of the deal I lose money, but if they back out, I get money. *We* get a lot of money that we could use for the Lodge."

"And I assume you have some sort of harebrained scheme to get them to back out?"

Chandler's grin grew. "Oh, do I ever."

-CHAPTER SIXTEEN-

LETTIE FELT BETTER with a warm cup of coffee nestled in her hands. Chandler was staring at her, but she wasn't ready to talk just yet. She took a slow sip of her drink and inhaled the scent of caramel and caffeine. Her emotions were a mess, vacillating between rage and the desire to help Chandler.

But one step at a time. She could handle that. Whatever she decided to do, she would need a plan and to make a good plan one needed all the facts. She took one more sip of her drink. "Okay, I'm ready to listen. Then I will make my decision."

The coffeeshop Chandler had led her to was quiet and was mostly deserted. Lettie and Chandler were tucked away in a corner, curled into overstuffed chairs. The irony of how cozy and content they must look to a passerby was not lost on Lettie.

"I could kiss you right now, Lettie Katz."

"Please control yourself." Though the desire to throttle Chandler was receding, Lettie still hadn't decided where she would land on the issue. The lie was enormous. "Just tell me your plan."

"So, here in Lilac Lake people aren't afraid of gorgons, but in the rest of the world there's a lot of prejudice. Maybe it's even well earned, we can turn people to stone."

"It's not like you or any other gorgon couldn't turn them back."

Chandler chuckled. "Well, let's not advertise that because we're going to play on that fear. The man who signed the contract, Alvin Condon, has always been fearful of me. He's extremely superstitious and distrustful of magic. Plus, he fired me."

"Then why would he buy a hotel in Lilac Lake?"

"The dollar signs. This town is beautiful, there's so much potential for a true tourist town here, even without the magic. But there's hardly an acre of land on the lake that someone doesn't own. So, the question is, can you stomach scamming a millionaire out of his barely worked for money?"

Lettie put her coffee down on the table between them. She was still furious with Chandler but owning the Lodge with her seemed better than owning it with some rich asshole. "I am not entirely opposed." A lifetime of friendship with Daphne and being raised by Monica had predisposed Lettie to all manner of subterfuge.

"And your friends? Do you think any of them would be willing to help out? You know this town better than I do."

Green magic swirled around Lettie. She knew this wasn't a prospect she should be excited about, but it sure beat being furious with Chandler. In fact, being mad at Chandler had always been hard for her. She welcomed having a task she could focus on. "Yeah, I think we could rope a few people in, as long as it's not dangerous. I don't want to hurt anyone."

"No, definitely not. We aren't actually going to hurt anyone. We're just going to make Alvin believe we could, that we might if things don't go our way. That will confirm his suspicions that this town is full of barely contained, extremely dangerous, magic. And, hopefully, he'll be too scared to stay and beg me to let him out of the contract."

"We did make a little explosion."

"That's my girl."

The words hit Lettie like a brick to the chest. *Chandler's girl.* What more had she wanted only an hour ago? She pushed past it. All of that could wait. The important thing was the Lodge and making sure that Lettie didn't co-own it with some bigoted man who only saw the monetary value of it and not all the ways it was beautiful.

But Chandler has clearly seen her discomfort. She picked up her chai latte and sunk deeper into her chair. "I really am sorry. I think what we have could be so good."

Lettie waved her hand, looking away from Chandler and through the window. How much longer before the cold set in completely for the season? "I'm not ready to talk about that." What she wanted to talk about was Gwen. She wanted to know every detail, let each one tear at her, comparing herself to someone she could never be. But what was the sense in that? Still, her willpower only went so far. "Gwen is staying at the Lodge?"

"I didn't know until today. Pepper must have made the reservation. You can't blame her."

"I don't," Lettie said through gritted teeth. "When is Alvin coming?"

"At the end of the week." Chandler's fingers made indents in the styrofoam cup.

Lettie stood up and put her hand out. "We'll keep the Lodge in the family."

Chandler stood and gripped her hand, her thumb brushing over Lettie's fingers and sending a thrill through her. "Can we talk more? I know you're upset, but I don't want things to be like this between us."

Magic sparked, hot embers that made them both pull back their hands. "No. Not right now. I'm still mad, I just don't want to lose something I've worked for."

"Okay. Whatever you need."

"I'll go rally the troops."

Maybe it was just Lettie's imagination, but outside the air seemed cooler, the promise of spring rescinded. The town had returned to winter, and she pulled her jacket tight around her.

She still needed groceries, but the idea of being alone with her thoughts in the unnaturally bright, slightly smelly grocery store was more than she could take. She tried to head back to the Lodge but for a moment her feet wouldn't move. Gwen must have made it there by now and Lettie didn't know how she would face her.

But that wasn't who she was. She didn't give up or roll over. The Lodge was hers; it had been hers from the moment she was born. It would not be another casualty of capitalism, and neither would she. She didn't want some corporate logo or standardization. To save her birthright, she could be a scary witch. For a decade she had convinced herself that was exactly what she was, how hard could it be to convince someone else?

She had a banshee for a roommate and siren friends. Oak was a shifter and Chandler was a gorgon. If Gwen and Alvin were scared of magic, she'd make them horrified. She'd send them running back to New York or wherever the fuck they were from. But the Lodge was, and always would be, hers.

"You want me to scare a man?" Daphne looked downright delighted at the prospect. "Hell yeah, I'm in."

"And we aren't mad at Chandler?" Lorne was perched on the arm of the couch, a beer dangling from his fingers.

"I'm not saying that we're happy with her." Lettie sipped her own beer. "I think a certain amount of anger is justified."

"And where is this Gwen? Did you check the computer?" Daphne stared at the door like Chandler's ex might walk through it at any minute. "She sounds like a real piece of work."

"I didn't check." Though she had thought about it. Lettie had let the mouse hover over the reservations tab for several minutes before thinking better of it and going to her room.

"We could hang out in the common area. You own this place. You have every right to be there."

"Yeah." Lorne got to his feet. "I want to see her. Come on, Lettie." He grabbed his sister's hands and pulled. "You loved playing spies when we were little."

"Oh, that's right. You were always taking me on stakeouts. That's how we found out my parents were getting divorced," Daphne said.

"I'm still really sorry about that."

"My heart has healed." She placed her hands, one on top of the other, on her chest and let out a mournful sigh.

"You're a real comedian." Lettie followed the two of them into the hallway, trying not to look at Chandler's door. Was she back from sweet talking Amelia?

A sudden urge to knock on the door overcame her, and she quickened her pace to follow the other two. She knew exactly what would happen if she set foot in that apartment, and she wasn't ready to forgive Chandler yet, or fall back into her bed. It would do Chandler some good to wallow a little longer.

Pepper was shoving things in her purse at the front desk. "Hey, boss. I was just about to head out. Andy just got here for the night."

Daphne leaned on the counter, "Quick question, a blonde woman checked in earlier. Do you know if she's still in the building?"

Pepper glanced towards Lettie. "I…"

"Ignore her." Lettie pulled on Daphne. "Quit harassing her."

Daphne pouted but obeyed and followed Lettie and Lorne to one of the expansive rooms that made up the front of the Lodge. There were a few people in the dining room, but Lettie settled into the parlor, running her fingers over the spines of books that filled the shelves.

The parlor had always been her favorite; each book felt like a treasure waiting to be discovered. Plus, she could overhear guests while they ate if it was quiet enough and she really had enjoyed playing spies as a kid.

But at that moment, it all felt silly. Even if Gwen came downstairs, what was Lettie going to say? She'd love to have some clever quip, but everything was still so fresh and Lettie had never possessed the quick tongue that Daphne did.

"We could seduce her and steal the contract."

"Daphne, shut up," Lorne said. "Look at Lettie. She's sad. We're supposed to be supportive. Do you want to go hit something? Eat some ice cream? Scream at the sky?"

"The third has merit." Lettie watched an older couple through the doorway. The woman was laughing, and the man swiped a piece of chicken off her plate grinning the whole time. "I wasn't even looking, you know. It's not like I was lonely. And now—"

"I'll be right back," Daphne kissed her head and then went into the dining room.

Lorne sat beside Lettie. "I'm not sure exactly what I'm supposed to be doing. I'm bad at this. But I'm here, for whatever you need, up to and including felonies."

"Oh yeah. Got something in mind?" Though Lorne was a disaster most of the time, Lettie appreciated that he was always there. Annoyingly so sometimes, but there.

Daphne returned carrying a large slice of chocolate cake and three forks. "Ms. Evette's cake fixes any ails."

Lorne took the cake and put it between them, but his eyes scanned the dining room. "She has to come out, eventually."

"Not really." Lettie grabbed a fork and sunk it into the rich chocolate. The first burst of flavor on her tongue did make her feel a little better. After all, she was half owner of the cake and all Lodge cakes. That had to count for something.

The older couple had finished their meal and made their way out of the dining room and into the parlor. They slowed when they noticed Lettie.

"The lovely woman running the desk said you own this place, dear," the woman said. Her smile was warm and made Lettie think of Hattie, the way she used to smile at customers like they were old friends.

"Oh, yes!" Lettie brought her hand to cover her mouth, trying not to spew cake on paying customers.

"We remember your grandmother well. We've been coming here for years. This was where we went for our first night away after my oldest was born, we stayed in one of the cabins. I'm thrilled to see they're being updated."

Daphne nudged Lettie's shoulder, grinning from ear to ear.

Unexpected tears formed in Lettie's eyes. "Thank you so much." She stood up, resisting the urge to hug the woman.

"Of course," the man said, patting her shoulder. "It's good to see a younger generation keeping up wonderful traditions like this. Our granddaughter married a siren this spring, and he seems like such a nice young man."

"Well, we won't keep you. But tell the chef the food is as wonderful as ever."

Lettie watched them disappear up the stairs to the guest rooms. "That was so nice."

"Gran would have loved that. I bet she knew their names and everything." Lorne shoveled more cake into his mouth.

"Lettie…" Daphne said, nudging her once again, but this time there was no grin. "Look."

-CHAPTER SEVENTEEN-

WITH A STEADYING breath, Lettie turned. But it wasn't Gwen waiting for her, it was Chandler. Lettie wasn't sure if that was better or worse, only that she wished she could have basked in the glory of old person praise a moment longer.

"Can I talk to you?" Chandler asked.

"Hmp." Daphne leaned back in her chair. "*Traitor.* And to think I tried to like you."

"Yes, we can talk," Lettie said, against her better judgment. She stood, but a growing awareness swirled inside her. Somewhere above them was Gwen, beautiful and poised. Was that what Chandler wanted? Someone so unlike Lettie.

She resented the thought. Who cared? Was Chandler even what *she* wanted? Aloof and prone to running away when things got tough. Not exactly the perfect woman.

But she followed that imperfect woman away from her friends, trying to get her emotions under control.

Chandler rounded a corner and pulled Lettie into a supply closet where the air was thick with the smell of lavender cleaning products.

"What are you doing? We both live here, we don't need to hide."

"I know, but I didn't think you'd come to my apartment. I just—shit, I should have prepared a speech or something." She took a step closer, and Lettie took a step back, but the space was limited.

Lettie knocked into a mop, and it clattered to the ground. "I'm so fucking mad at you. And jealous! It's like the dumbest thing in the world to feel jealous when I should be furious. I should want to rip your face off, but instead I keep thinking about Gwen. She's like—like a fucking bitchy barbie or something. And I hate that I keep thinking about you and her. That you were so enamored by her you were willing to sell this place, everything our grandmothers worked for. But of course you are! Who wouldn't be, she's beautiful and—"

Chandler's mouth crashed into Lettie's, her tongue sweeping through her mouth, claiming her. "*You're* beautiful." She held Lettie's face in her hands. "You're so beautiful and perfect and everything I want. You're so incredible I had to run away to get free of you. I knew if I stayed I'd never leave this town. I didn't care about the explosion, I didn't care if we blew up the entire state of Virginia. But I should have stayed. There's nothing out there I need—girls that make me forget for a night, a month, whatever. Nothing important."

Lettie's head was only static with no coherent thoughts. "Those are just words."

"I know. *I know.* And I am going to fix this. I'm going to make it better. I promise." Her words came out in a breathless jumble. "Fuck, Lettie." She kissed her again, pressing her back into the metal shelves.

Lettie pushed her away. "You can say all that but obviously you wanted her. Look at what you did. You sold the business without even telling me." And maybe it was easier to focus on Gwen, on jealousy, than think about how Chandler had lied, over and over. How she had broken Lettie's heart again.

"I didn't do it because of her. Sure, I was sad. Everyone's sad when they get dumped, but it was still about you. I saw you in that lawyer's office and I wanted to kiss you then, just like I have every time I've ever seen you. And I was scared to stay."

"That doesn't make me feel better." But Lettie yearned to reach for her, pull her closer, kiss her again. God, she was an idiot. She should be screaming. "I want to be here. In Lilac Lake. I want this. The Lodge, the town, a place with my family and friends. I don't want to leave. And I thought I wanted you, but not if you're going to lie to me. Not if it's going to be like this."

"It won't. I was going to tell you after I met with her. I just wanted to get out of it first. I knew within days I had screwed up. I didn't tell you because I was never going to let Alvin have the Lodge." Chandler reached for her.

This time Lettie didn't move away. "It was still a lie."

"I was a chickenshit. Too afraid of seeing the disappointment in your eyes. I didn't want you to stop smiling. And I'm sorry. You deserved better." Chandler lowered her head and kissed the hollow of Lettie's throat then trailed kisses further down her chest.

It took everything in Lettie not to give in completely, not to close her eyes and let Chandler continue her descent, but she wrapped her hands about Chandler's face and pulled her up. "Chandler, what is this?"

"I'm not good at this part, Lettie. I never have been."

"And how has that worked? We own a business. Or we were supposed to." Lettie brushed the hair away from Chandler's face, feeling the almost familiar pull of her darkness, the swirling abyss inside her. As frustrated as she was, she could understand Chandler's decision, the panic she must have felt when she found out she was supposed to run the Lodge with her ex in a town she hadn't called home in a decade. "We have things to work out—about us, about the Lodge. Fucking won't fix any of it."

"Okay, yeah." Chandler took a deep breath. "I can do this. It's just talking, right?"

The words were clearly not for Lettie so she kept her mouth shut, waiting to hear whatever Chandler would say and enjoying the way her cheeks turned pink.

"I'm falling for you, Lettie Katz. You make me feel things that, when I was young, I wished I didn't, and that I'm still scared of, but I want them. I want them with you. You feel like home—the way home is supposed to feel. And so, I want to give this thing between us a chance. A real chance. You and me. Do you want that too? Please don't say no, because that's the nicest thing I've ever said to anyone."

"Yes," Lettie laughed. "I absolutely do want that. As long as you mean it."

Chandler grabbed Lettie around the waist and tried to twirl her, an impossible task in such a small space. "Yes, of course I mean it. I don't just say things like that. It made my stomach hurt." She kissed Lettie again, tangling her fingers in her hair, but Lettie pulled back.

"I have to be able to trust you. Really trust you. And I'm a forgiving person, but I'm not a fool. Not even for you."

"Yes. Absolutely. I'm working on myself. And not just for you, but because I'm so damn tired of being a disaster. I want to be stable, make a life I can be proud of instead of leaving a trail of smoking wreckage everywhere I go." Chandler smiled, most of the panic out of her eyes. "I really want to kiss you more."

A small ember of hope burned in Lettie's chest, even while she promised herself that what she said was true. She wouldn't be a fool, not even for Chandler. She'd guard her heart until the gorgon had earned it. But that didn't mean she had to guard *all* of herself. "I am not fucking you in this supply closet. We literally own this place. We have beds."

"To bed it is." Chandler reached down, threading her fingers through Lettie's. "Does this mean we should tell the town about us?"

"Chandler, are you asking to be my *girlfriend?*"

"Gross. Maybe. We can discuss." She turned as she pushed the door open and continued to kiss Lettie, running her hands down her thighs. "Ugh. Come on. Hurry. Forget your friends. They'll figure it out."

Lettie hadn't even been thinking of them. "You're the one slowing us down. Come on, snake girl!" She grabbed Chandler's hand and rushed into the hallway giggling like a teenager.

And almost crashed right into Gwen.

The woman looked the two of them over. She was out of her suit, and in a pair of jeans that probably cost more than all the jeans Lettie owned combined. "Chandler. Lettie."

"Gwen." Chandler's grip on Lettie's hand tightened. "My offer still stands. We can make this easy and void the agreement."

"Because you're horny for some hometown girl?" Gwen sneered.

"Oh, *absolutely* not." Lettie did her best to channel her inner Daphne and straightened her spine, bringing herself up to her full height. "Nope. Not in my Lodge."

"Excuse me?"

"You heard me just fine. I know my accent isn't that strong, even for a hometown girl. Go pack your bags. You can stay somewhere else tonight. I'll refund your payment."

"You can't do that. I paid for a night. I'll be staying for a night."

Lettie let her magic gather around her, sparkling in the air and casting an eerie green glow down the hallway. She was loath to let go of Chandler's hand, but she pulled away and put her hands on her hips. "You think so? What are you going to do? Call the cops? Go ahead." She pulled her phone from her pocket and held it out.

Gwen made a motion like she wanted to straighten a blazer that wasn't there. "Fine." She turned her gaze to Chandler. "But when this fails do not come knocking on my door. Do you remember all those times when you cried because they passed you over for promotion? This is why, however you want to act, you've always been—"

"Hey!" Daphne's voice echoed through the space, making Lettie's ears ring. "The lady asked you to leave. Now you can leave just as you are, or you can leave with bleeding eardrums." She took a step closer, her power glowing white hot across her skin.

Gwen blanched, and Lettie almost felt bad. "Whatever. This changes nothing, Chandler. You signed a contract." She turned and the three of them watched her go.

"Making out in small spaces again?" Daphne pursed her lips. "Go ahead. I'll take care of Lorne."

Once again, Lettie wasn't even going to ask. She laced her fingers back through Chandler's and pulled her towards the doorway to their apartments. "Is she…always like that?"

"It was a lot better when she didn't hate me. Plus, I turned her down at the diner which didn't help."

"You turned her down?"

Chandler pushed the door to the apartment hallway open. Overhead the fluorescent lights flickered. "Of course. I'm not that kind of girl, Katz."

"Oh, yes, you are." Lettie turned the knob to Chandler's apartment.

Each time she went inside there were changes, little bits that made it seem more and more like Chandler's home and not somewhere she was subletting. Her leather jacket draped across a chair, more art on the walls that Everly would have never approved of, a little container of colorful kitchenware.

"I'm reformed. A reformed rake." She nuzzled against Lettie's neck and kicked the door shut. "Take your clothes off."

Lettie pulled her shirt over her head and shimmied down her pants. "What now?"

The gorgon's stare was penetrating. Lettie could feel it, vibrating over her skin. Chandler pulled Lettie to her, tugging at her earlobe with her teeth. "Bed. Now."

"Okay." Lettie's voice was breathless, and she obeyed, lowering herself slowly onto Chandler's bed while she watched. "Like this?" She ran her hand down her chest and onto her stomach. She was already wet, her core heated and yearning for the gorgon.

Chandler undressed, revealing her full breasts and the curve where her waist slimmed, and all the parts Lettie wanted to touch so desperately. She prowled onto the bed, situating herself between Lettie's thighs and ran her hands up them. "Perfect." She crawled further up, pressing their bodies together. "I have been aching for you all day. Do you want to taste me, Lettie?"

More than she could stand. "I'm so mad at you, still."

"I know." Chandler ran her thumb along Lettie's lips. "Furious. But you still want me, don't you?"

"Yes." Lettie grabbed Chandler, pushed her onto the bed, and gazed down at every perfect inch of her before kissing her roughly, dragging her lips between her teeth. She had lied to her. So many times. Lettie slid her hand between Chandler's legs, avoiding the spot she knew Chandler wanted her to touch. "I'm not going to taste you."

"No?" Now it was Chandler's turn to be breathless. More words formed at her lips and were driven away with a gasp when Lettie pushed her fingers inside of her.

Chandler's back arched off the bed, and she gripped the sheets as Lettie drove her fingers inside of her and grasped her breast, twisting Chandler's nipple between her fingers. She pressed further into the gorgon and pulled out slowly, again and again until Chandler was panting.

She gripped a handful of Lettie's hair, yanking her down. "Do you forgive me?"

"Not yet." Lettie swiped her thumb over Chandler's clit. "Tell me again you want me."

"I want you," she bit out, struggling with each word as Lettie continued circling her core.

"Stop talking." Lettie pulled her hand away from Chandler. "And fuck me."

"Gladly." Chandler gripped her by her waist, urging Lettie upward and Lettie settled herself over Chandler's mouth, gripping the headboard with both hands.

She rode Chandler as the gorgon's tongue slid over her, inside her, her hands never leaving Lettie's waist, her fingernails dug into soft flesh as Lettie bucked against her.

She threw her head back and closed her eyes, her whole world reduced down to the feeling of the woman underneath her, licking her so thoroughly. When she came, she screamed, and the sound carried away some of her frustration.

Chandler released her only long enough to push her down onto the bed and crawled onto top of her. She reached for Lettie's throat, a gentle pressure as she aligned their bodies together. "Do you forgive me?"

"No." Lettie slapped Chandler's hand away and pulled her nipple into her mouth, swirling her tongue over the hardened peak before dragging her teeth along the sensitive skin. Then she leaned back, crossing her hands behind her head, watching Chandler as she fucked her. "But I'm close."

"Me too."

The room was sweltering. Lettie waved her hand and the window swung open, rewarding them with a cool breeze that washed across Lettie's sweat slick skin.

"Sometimes it sounds like the wind is singing to me, like words are running through the leaves and if I'm silent enough I can hear them." Lettie didn't know why she said it, except she was tired of holding her magic close.

Chandler kissed her softly. "That's how I feel with the snakes sometimes. They listen to me, I can control them in a way, but sometimes it feels like if I only tried a little harder I could understand them too."

Lettie rolled over in bed and propped her hand on her head. "I am so nervous right now. All I can think of is all the ways this could go wrong. Even if we get you out of the contract, is this thing between us the smart thing to do? Who knows how things will look in a year. And we'll still have the Lodge to run."

Chandler placed her hand over her heart. "I swear if this goes wrong between us I will do the right thing and become a silent partner until you can buy me out. That's what I should have done in the first place. I was just…I don't know. Coming back here, seeing you. I felt like a teenager again."

"Well, you handled it really well. I liked when you told me to shut the fuck up in the lawyer's office."

Chandler pulled Lettie close. "I am nothing if not poised." She kissed Lettie softly. "I really don't want to fuck this up."

Well, don't. But Lettie knew it wasn't that simple. There was so much that could go wrong, so many differences between them. Right now, everything was hot and heavy. What would happen when the drama and novelty wore off? Did they have what it took to make a relationship last?

Unfortunately, she could think of nothing to say, no simple platitude to make Chandler laugh, and the moment stretched between them. Some of the joy fell from Chandler's face and Lettie kissed her again, unsure of what else to do. "When does Alvin come?"

"Saturday." Chandler slid out of bed. "I'll fix this, Lettie. I—god, this is so corny, but coming back here, all of this, it feels right. Like I've finally found where I'm supposed to be." She pulled on a pair of leggings, doing a little dance to work them up over her ass.

"I believe you. And I also believe that between the five of us we can terrify a man into leaving town."

"That's the spirit."

-CHAPTER EIGHTEEN-

LETTIE'S SKIN WAS still tingling when left Chandler's apartment and stepped into the hallway. She needed a shower, to eat something with some protein or at least a vitamin in it. Unfortunately, before she could make it across the hall and to her own apartment, the door at the end of the hall swung open, and her mother stepped through, carrying a cup of coffee.

"Well, there's my little baby. How have you been?" Monica kissed her on the cheek and then opened Lettie's door without invitation. "Come on."

Lettie had little choice but to follow, it was her house after all. "Hello, mother."

"I guess it's true then." She settled into a floral armchair.

"I guess it is." Lettie had no idea what Monica was talking about. She poured herself a glass of water and sat on the couch.

"When were you planning on telling me?" Monica crossed one yoga pants clad leg over the other.

"Oh, really soon. What exactly are we talking about though?" Lettie made a mental list of things she needed to do, starting with putting a lock on the hallway leading to their apartments and never giving her mother a key.

"You and Chandler. Vonetta Murphy called me last night. Said she saw you two at the bar. Now, why wouldn't you tell your mother?"

Fuck. "We haven't told anyone—"

"Lorne sure knew, so I guess you've told someone. Just not me."

Lettie tried to keep the irritation off her face, but she was going to strangle her brother. "Mom." She put down the glass of water and folded her hands together. "I was absolutely going to tell you before I told anyone else, I just hadn't had time to call you yet. But, hey! What do you think about all this development in Lilac Lake? I'm worried about where it's all headed." The perfect distraction.

"Oh, Lettie, you know I hate it. None of them are from here. All these outsiders have no idea what they're doing. Remember that new coffee shop? Tasted like ass. Those idiots can't even brew a cup of coffee. How can they run a business?"

"Well…can I tell you something? But you have to promise you won't tell Ginger. Seriously, it's a secret until Chandler talks to her."

Monica leaned closer, brushing her bleached blonde hair over her shoulder. "Of course, I came here first instead of calling her. I wanted to ask you first. I do try."

"I know, mom. So, the thing is, Chandler signed something she shouldn't have, and we need to get her out of a contract with some conglomerate. And it turns out the buyer is a little scared of magic, especially the kind we have in Lilac Lake. I was hoping you might help us?"

The chance of her mother doing anything to actually help was extremely low, but if there was anything Monica Katz loved more than gossip and daytime soaps, it was shenanigans. And she'd rather talk about her mother's hatred of anyone she deemed an outsider than listen to her opinions on Chandler.

"Of course I'll help," Monica said, "I assume you've already told Daphne. She's got a head for these things."

"She is a banshee."

"Some girls have all the luck. Have you seen the target? I assume he's older. I'll do some scouting and see what I can learn about him. But I really think you and Chandler should tell Ginger. She'd be good at this. Plus, she'll be so thrilled, Letts."

"Mom, we just wanted to figure things out for ourselves first. Between our past and the Lodge, everything is really complicated."

"I know, honey." Monica patted Lettie's hand. "I remember when I first met your dad. Oh, his parents hated me. We'd sneak out to the lake just to be together and watch the sunset. He knew all the constellations.

I miss him all the time, Lettie. He'd be so proud of you. Probably Lorne too." She smirked.

Lettie laughed. "I miss him too." The truth was, she barely remembered her father except in hazy memories of laughter, of being held on shoulders, and scratchy bearded kisses. Still, she missed him in her own way—all the things he had missed, all the times she had wished for another parent, all her envy of little girls who did not even know what they had. "How come you never worked for the inn?"

Her mother waved her hand like she was swatting a fly. "Oh, I did here and there. But this job wasn't for me. Now, tell me sweetheart, are you happy? I know she made it hard for you sometimes when you were little. I don't think she knew how to act around you, or anybody for that matter. Like I said, she's a sweet girl, but she never had good control over her magic, always turning toads and lizards to stone. A bird once. It frightened her mother."

Lettie wasn't sure she wanted to hear any of this. She'd struggled with her own magic too, but no one had ever noticed until she blew up town square. Did she wish they had? "Yeah, I think I am happy. I'll be happier once everything is settled. Once the construction is done."

"Oh, of course. And I've heard about the little festival you want to plan. Let me know if I can help out with that."

They both looked up at the sound of Daphne emerging from her bedroom. "Hey Monica. Coffee?" Her eyes were barely open as she headed towards the kitchen.

"Sure. Lettie was catching me up on your little plan."

Daphne froze, turning slowly. "Oh?" Her face lit up, and she bounced on her toes. "Oh! Yeah. This really dials it up." She pulled the cold brew out of the fridge and turned towards Lettie. "You have to talk to Chandler because if Ginger gets involved too, we can't lose. My mom still talks about their senior prank. They couldn't even get into the school."

"Those were the days." Monica sighed, smiling. "So, girls, let's come up with some ideas."

There was little to do around the Lodge until construction was done, leaving Lettie feeling like she was forgetting an important task. But everything was running smoothly, the renovations were coming along, reservations were rolling in, and while things with Chandler were still tense, she felt okay.

But in two days Alvin Condon would be there, and she still wasn't sure how she wanted to play things. Sweet? Lead him into a false sense of security? Salty? That had to be what he was expecting.

The thought of some man in her Lodge—running his eyes over the furniture, making mental lists of what he wanted to change—made her want to throw up.

And that led to frustration at Chandler, at how rash and thoughtless she had been, how little she had cared about the legacy their families had built. And was that someone she wanted to build a relationship with?

But then she'd look at her, watch her stop to pick up a snake or curl up to read in the chairs near the windows, sunlight threading through her hair, and it was so hard to be mad.

She'd apologized until Lettie asked her to stop and promised repeatedly that if things didn't work out between them, she'd step back. She promised she had learned her lesson. She would be a silent partner until Lettie could buy her out.

But Lettie hated that too. She'd watched her Gran and Everly work together her whole life, watched them laugh and argue. She wanted that—someone to share the load with. Maybe if Chandler left, she'd ask Daphne to buy her out, or Amelia. Anyone that wouldn't leave Lettie running the Stone and Sorcery alone.

"What's with the thinking face?" Chandler wrapped her arms around Lettie's waist.

"Just nervous." Lettie felt the pull of magic, her own and Chandler's, something she had never felt before with anyone. Often, she wondered if it meant something. She'd been aware of other magic, the pull of a siren like a string around her heart, the rattling uncertainty of the banshee, the primal urge of the shifter, but never deep inside her like this, not just washing over her but ingraining itself into her core. "Can you feel me? My magic?"

"Yeah." Chandler kissed her forehead. "You're like…" She chewed on her lip, thinking. "Like spring, when everything gets warm and there's hope in the air. A promise that things will bloom again."

Oh. She'd never thought of herself like that. "That might be the nicest thing anyone's ever said to me."

"Happy to oblige. Do you want to get lunch? I was thinking something greasy, french fries, maybe even onion rings?" She wiggled her eyebrows.

"Oh, tell me more." Lettie pretended to swoon.

Chandler moved closer, and her breath brushed against the shell of Lettie's ear. She lowered her voice, dark and husky. "Smoked meats. Corn dogs. Milkshakes. Cobb salad."

The last one was too much, and Lettie burst out laughing. "Yeah, sure. Hershel's it is."

The day was still young, and the diner was mostly empty. The rich aroma of coffee and grease hit Lettie's nose as soon as she opened the door and headed to her usual booth.

Herschel was behind the counter, wiping it to a shine, and smiled at Lettie as she came in. "The Lodge is looking great. I saw them working when I was in the boat the other day."

"That boat still working?" Lettie slid into the booth.

"You sound like your mama. Anneliese will be with you in just a moment. Good to see you, Chandler."

Chandler grinned, leaning across the booth as Hershel disappeared behind the employees only door. "We're making progress. He usually doesn't even acknowledge I'm here."

"You'll be back in the swing of it in no time." Lettie looked up at the waitress's approach and ordered a Cobb salad, she couldn't get them out of her mind, and a water.

When Anneliese left, she busied herself straightening out the sugar packets. "So, I think we kind of charm him at first. We want Condon to trust us, right? What do you think?"

Chandler pulled Lettie's hand away from the sugar and wrapped it in her own. "Yeah, that's what I was thinking too."

"Weird question, but does he like women? And how old is he?"

"Um, yes and mid-fifties, I think. I feel obligated to ask...why?"

"Well, I've been putting off telling you this, but my mom knows—she hasn't told Ginger—but she thinks maybe she could soften him up, do a little fact finding. And that should keep her busy, so she doesn't come up with anything more sinister."

There was a long pause before Chandler spoke. She pulled her hands away, but not before Lettie could feel her stony fingertips brush across her palms and ran her hand through her hair. "I should talk to my mom."

"Yeah, probably. But my mom really didn't tell her anything. I would have told you sooner if I thought she had."

Chandler looked Lettie over like she was looking for cracks, then she nodded. "Of course. And yeah, I think Alvin would be quite susceptible to your mother's charms."

"It's just your mom, Chandler. Do you want to call her? You can invite her to lunch."

"You don't want to have lunch with my mother."

"I've had more lunches with your mom than you have. Look, it's your choice, completely your choice…"

Chandler's phone was already in her hand. "No. I'm doing it. I'm doing it. Right? I'm doing it? I'm telling my mom a real thing about my life."

"You'll feel better once it's done. Like pulling off a band aid." Lettie had the strongest desire to walk around the table, slip into the booth, and hold Chandler, but she stayed in her seat. She knew this was something the gorgon needed to do on her own. "She's really not so bad. I mean, she's a lot, but she loves you."

"Okay." Chandler nodded and put the phone to her ear. "Hey mom, you busy?"

Fifteen minutes later, Ginger burst into the diner. Her salt and pepper curls were blown out, and her heels clacked with each step. "Baby!" Chandler stood and Ginger pulled her into a hug. "And Lettie. Look at you girls!" She sat down beside Lettie and kissed her on the cheek.

"Hey Ginger. How's the salon going?"

"Oh, fantastic! To be honest, I'm always relieved when the tourists leave. I feel like I'm a chicken with my head cut off when they're here. I barely have time to breathe." She took a fry from Chandler's plate. "Now, you must have something important to tell me to call me out of the blue. You've been here for weeks, but I've barely seen you."

Chandler stared hard at her burger before finally dragging her gaze up to look at her mother. There was so much resemblance between the two of them, the same sharp features, the curly dark hair. "There's something I wanted to tell you, mom, and I wanted you to hear it from me."

"Well, if you're about to tell me you're gay I'm afraid that ship has sailed a long time ago, sweetling." Ginger winked.

"I'm—" Chandler took a deep breath and the fork in her hand turned to stone.

"Goodness, baby. Did something happen?"

"No. No, it's good mom. I think it's really good. I'm going to stay here for a while, settle down. Settle down with Lettie."

Ginger blinked, while Lettie's stomach felt like Chandler had just shoved her stony fist straight into it. Settle down? She wanted to settle down with Lettie? But the dread quickly receded, replaced with warmth like she'd just taken a deep drink of tea. Of all the ways Chandler could tell her mother she'd chosen that. To settle down with Lettie.

"You want…." Ginger blinked again. "Chandler Hart, are you dating Lettie?" Ginger turned towards Lettie, her blue eyes wide. "The two of you?" Lettie nodded. "Well, I'll be! That is excellent news. Hershel, bring me a milkshake. I've got something to celebrate!"

The blush spreading across Chandler's face was the deepest red Lettie had ever seen and went all the way to her hairline. "You aren't mad?"

"Mad? Why would I be mad? I'm fixin' to run right out of here and phone Monica. My baby is staying here, and she's got herself the sweetest girlfriend in five counties. I'm just pleased as punch, Channy. Pleased as punch."

Lettie suppressed her giggles. She forgot how southern Ginger got when she was really and truly excited. "So, my mom does know, but she just found out. And you're going to have a lot to talk about because we've got a little something planned. A little…"

"We're trying to scam a man, mama. I did something idiotic, and we just need to scare him."

"Well, your father has a shotgun if—"

"Not like that. Definitely not like that. We're thinking something a little less…felonious."

"The old boys in blue haven't caught me yet." Ginger laughed. "Now, you two are going to tell me everything."

-CHAPTER NINETEEN-

THERE WASN'T ANYTHING left to do. Lettie had straightened everything she could straighten, she'd dusted surfaces that were already clean, she'd eaten at least two too many crullers. Soon Alvin Condon would be there.

She glanced over her shoulder. Pepper was refilling a little glass dish of mints. They'd only told her the bare minimum about what was going on, but Lettie could see the tension in her shoulders. Pepper didn't want a stranger running the Lodge. She didn't want to deal with corporate rules and people who wouldn't let her take weeks off to go visit her sister when she had a baby or let her stay at the Lodge for free when her apartment flooded.

In an effort to take Pepper's mind off of the possible change in management, Lettie had brought the contractor in and told him she could design her office however she wanted.

But she wished she hadn't told Pepper anything at all. There was nothing she could do to help, she was human, and besides, this wasn't her fight. Whatever happened, she'd have a job. She'd always have a job at the Stone and Sorcery.

Pepper glanced up at Lettie. "I'm okay," she mouthed.

All Lettie had to do was breathe. She'd met Gwen and Condon couldn't be worse than she was.

The grandfather clock struck noon, and the door swung open. Lettie forced a smile onto her face while her stomach did the Charleston. The man who walked in was tall and slim, handsome in a rich, white, over-privileged sort of way. Decidedly human, not a wisp of magic anywhere around him.

"You must be Mr. Condon." Lettie smiled and put out her hand.

It shook it. "Call me Alvin. Lettie Katz, I presume? Hotelier?"

Hotelier? As if. "That's me. Chandler is waiting in the dining room. Lunch service just started a half hour ago if you're hungry."

"I could eat."

As Lettie led him towards the dining room and past a nauseated looking but grinning Pepper, she felt like she was in the start of a heist movie. She was glad Alvin couldn't hear her heartbeat because it thumped in her chest, pumping adrenaline through her body. The thought of scaring this man into abandoning the contract—of pulling off shenanigans with Chandler—both excited and terrified her.

There was a sparkle in Chandler's eye when she stood at their approach. "Alvin, how have you been?" She pulled out his chair.

He sat, shook out his napkin, and placed it in his lap. "I've been better, Chandler. I hated to hear how things went down between you and Gwen."

Lettie sat between them and grabbed a roll out of the wicker basket in the middle of the table, biding her time.

"I hear you," Chandler said. "You know how she and I are, oil and water. I apologize for my outburst. But I think we can all find a way to work together. And I'm certain you'll find that Lettie is a wonderful business partner."

Alvin pivoted towards her. "I do hope so, Lettie. I know this may not have been what you had in mind for your grandmother's Lodge, but once you hear my proposals, I think you'll come around. I have a lot of experience in these things, and this is a cute little town, just waiting to be discovered. Plus, I've been wanting to expand into the paranormal sector so it's an opportunity for both of us."

Chandler shot Lettie a look. "Well, we've got plenty of paranormal here. They say the lake is the source of all the strange magic in this town. Lettie has talked about playing that up."

"We'll have to row out there sometime. It's quite exhilarating to feel all that magic…though I'm not sure if it would be quite the same for you." Lettie took a sip of her sweet tea, surveying Alvin over the rim of the glass.

"Perhaps." Alvin glanced around the dining room. "And does the Lodge usually cater to supernatural or normal guests?"

Normal. She hated him already. "A mix of both. Of course, the normal guests usually want a bit of a show. We always recommend the Three Sisters, it's a local bar owned by a siren. She and her sisters put on a performance most Saturdays. Nothing to actually control you, but you get an idea of their magic."

He looked like he was going to crawl out of his skin. "And people enjoy that?" He nodded at the server who sat plates with a sampling of the day's options in front of them.

"Oh, they love it. The squeamish don't usually come to Lilac Lake. I think it's good for smaller tourist destinations like ours to have a 'thing.' It really draws people in."

"Well, you seem to have a clear vision for this establishment, Ms. Katz. I really appreciate that in a partner."

They finished their lunch with Alvin complimenting the food, even though he barely ate anything. He was a professional man, but seemed to have very little heart, and was definitely afraid of supes. He nodded along to everything Lettie said while his eyes scanned the room as though something might jump out at him.

Once during the meal, Lettie had almost pretended she thought the Lodge was haunted, had been constructing a ghost story in her head, but decided to keep that one in her back pocket. She figured Lorne would love to help set up a fake haunting in one of the rooms.

Lettie got up from the table, forcing a smile onto her face, and tried not to look at Chandler too much, lest they give the plan away. "Now that you're fed, I'd love to show you around the grounds. Let you see what you're paying for." Lettie motioned towards the front door.

"Absolutely." Alvin brushed crumbs off his suit and followed Lettie.

She wished she had a moment alone with Chandler, long enough to run her hands down her sides, remember she was real, that she planned to stay, because right now Alvin and his interest in the Lodge seemed too real, too immediate.

As though she could sense Lettie's thoughts, Chandler moved forward, brushing their shoulders together, barely a touch, but it slowed Lettie's increasing heart rate.

Outside the air was chilled, and the sun struggled to shine through the overcast sky. It emboldened Lettie, as if Lilac Lake itself didn't want the man there, didn't want to lose its charm, to give in to tourist shops sell goods made anywhere but town, big hotels blocking out the views, and outsiders who didn't even try to understand what made the people who lived there special.

If this were a real tour, she would stop at the cabins, show him the ones that were halfway finished, all the special details she had chosen, the beautiful woodworking Lorne had done. Instead, she headed straight for the shore of the Lake.

"I wanted to bring you here first, show you what makes people fall in love with Lilac Lake. Lilac Lake is, of course, the official name of the lake, after all the lilacs that grow in the surrounding woods, but many people call it Siren Lake." Lettie glanced towards Chandler.

"But that is a misnomer, too," Chandler said. "Lilac Lake is just like any other magical place, full of all kinds of supes. There are plenty of towns where the majority of the supernaturals are shifters, or cities with fae. Some have many varieties, and witches tend to be anywhere that magic lives. But Lilac Lake, like few other places, created unique magic; gorgons, sirens and banshees—or at least that's what we were called when they had no other name for us. But however you view the magic of this town, it is a darker magic. A dangerous magic."

"So, when people learned about the magic in this town, they thought of those legends we've all heard of. They saw the lake and the alluring supes who live here and believed it must be sirens. But the magic of the lake fuels us all," Lettie smiled, genuinely proud of her town and how it had embraced the unusual people that lived there.

"Interesting. And—"

"Lettie!" Her mother rushed towards them, her blonde hair streaming behind her.

Oh, good lord. Was it time for Monica already?

"I was just looking for you," she said. "Well, hello. And who are you?" She fluttered her eyelashes and extended her hand. Though Lettie doubted her mother's charms would be the deciding factor in what Alvin did, it would be fun to watch—if a little skeevy. It would also give him one more reason to want to get out of this town when things took a turn.

Alvin took her hand in his with gentle fingers. "Alvin Condon. Are you one of the guests?"

"Oh, no." Monica giggled. "I'm Monica Katz, Lettie's mother. It's such a pleasure to meet you, Mr. Condon. I've heard we were expecting a visitor."

"The pleasure is all mine, Mrs. Katz."

"Oh, call me Monica. So how are you liking it?"

Chandler pulled a face behind Alvin's back, her green eyes wide with suppressed laughter.

"This is quite an interesting little town." Alvin looked Monica up and down.

Okay, maybe this was *all* skeevy because Lettie wanted to pluck his eyeballs out of his head. Or her eyeballs. Either way, somebody's eyeballs had to go.

But Monica was all smiles. "Say, do you have a moment? I've lived here my whole life. I could show you around. I'm sure my little Lettie is awfully busy."

"That would certainly be a treat, but I'm afraid your daughter had the same idea."

"Oh, go ahead." Lettie grinned. "You're in town for a week, right? We've got plenty of time. Might as well get to know the locals."

"See?" Monica brushed her hand along his forearm. "Come on. I know where to get the best coffee."

"Well, so far so good," Chandler said as soon as they were out of earshot. "But he's always been an idiot for a pretty woman. He was one of Gwen's first clients. She had no idea what she was doing but…"

"This isn't wrong, is it? I mean, it feels kind of wrong, but that might be because I just saw my mom flirting with someone. Also, I don't know what her plan actually is, and I'm scared it might involve stabbing."

"Assuming there's no stabbing, I'd say it's a gray area. Wrong? Right? Who's to say? But that man makes more in a day than the Lodge will earn in a year."

"I don't want to work with him." Lettie looked out at the lake, where the water was still, and magic called from the island. "But I'm also not sure how to stop being mad at you."

Chandler bent down and picked up a rock. She turned it over and ran her fingers along the surface. "The one thing I can't change." She threw the stone across the water, and it skipped, leaving ripples in its wake. "I know, Lettie. I wish there was something I could say to undo all of this."

Lettie wished she could let it go, just move on. But that had never been who she was. "This is a bad idea, you know. We're business partners. We shouldn't be sleeping together." And wouldn't it be simpler if all the felt was anger? If she didn't also long to reach out and touch Chandler, if even the mere inches between them didn't seem like too far to be apart?

"Do you want to stop?" Chandler picked up another rock, and the grass rustled. A green snake poked its head up, testing the air with its tongue before settling at her feet.

"I don't." Lettie sighed, sticking her hands in her back pockets. "But I'm afraid. I'm putting my heart and my livelihood in the same basket."

Chandler turned towards Lettie, her eyes blazing, wide and earnest. "There are a lot of promises I could make that I shouldn't, and I can't swear I'll never break your heart, that's an impossible promise, though I'll try my hardest. But I won't hurt your business. I know the Lodge is yours and that I'm just lucky enough to have had a piece handed to me."

Lettie tingled with magic, and the snake looked up, watching her. "Do you think our grandmothers planned this? I mean why else wouldn't she have told me unless she knew I'd get worked up ahead of time instead of being open-minded?"

"Oh, was that what you were at first? Open-minded?" Chandler smirked. "Come on." She threw an arm around Lettie's shoulder. "And yes. No one schemed better than the two of them, and no one was more furious than Everly when I took off. She was fuming because I made you cry."

That surprised Lettie. She knew Everly had been upset when Chandler left, but she hadn't known any of her indignation had been on Lettie's behalf. "I'm not sure I'm going to be very good at scaring anybody."

"I know. You're a gentle soul." Chandler squeezed her. "Luckily for you, I'm not. You know if it doesn't work out, I could actually turn him to stone. We'd save a ton of money on decorations with genuine human statues."

"Yeah, and it wouldn't be suspicious at all."

-CHAPTER TWENTY-

HALF THE PEOPLE Lettie knew were gathered in her living room.

Amelia was sitting in the window nook, her feet curled up under her, red hair blazing in the setting sun. Her brother and Daphne were on the couch, laughing at something that only made sense to the two of them, and Chandler was on the bar counter, between the kitchen and the living room, her feet dangling above the floor, a beer in her hand.

"I like this. It feels like a secret meeting. Like we're in a movie or something," Lorne said.

"It *is* a secret meeting, dumbass." Daphne grinned and reached across Lorne to grab her beer.

"I was thinking," Amelia said, "and it's not illegal to use siren powers in certain conditions. It's perfectly legal for self-defense, for consensual entertainment purposes, or other consensual practices that could not be construed as dangerous."

"Jesus, Amelia. Did you digest the lawbook?" Lorne twisted on the couch to look at her.

"I run a business, *dumbass*. It's my job to know the law."

"If y'all don't stop calling me dumbass I'm going to leave, and I'm an integral part of the group. I represent the men."

"A historically underrepresented demographic, yes." Chandler raised her beer bottle in a mock toast.

"You need to know how our minds work." He tapped his finger on his temple. "Get inside our head. That's what I offer to all of you. Free of charge."

"And what an honor it is." Lettie resisted the urge to smack him on the back of the head. Lorne was like the orange cat that used to live near the cabins when she was a kid, not many thoughts, often lost or confused, but well meaning.

The door opened and Ginger and Monica came in. A bottle of vivid green premixed margaritas sloshed under Monica's arm.

"Hello, sweetlings!" Monica chirped, putting the bottle down and sitting between Daphne and Lorne on the couch. "Hey, baby."

Ginger looked between Chandler and Lettie, then walked over to her daughter. "See what you've been missing. Community. Crime."

"More like I brought it here." Chandler picked up the bottle of margarita mixed and frowned at the ingredients list.

"No way, don't think like that," Monica said. "We've had developers sniffing around here for years now. You screwed up, but this fight is going to keep happening. We've got to make sure they don't get a foothold on the lake though."

"Because of the magic?" Amelia asked, moving from her window seat.

"Because I'll be damned if our beautiful lake has some mega-hotel on it. It'll look like shit," Monica said. "Marg me, Ginger."

"Coming right up." Ginger headed towards the kitchen cabinets and started rifling through them.

This was feeling less like a secret meeting and more like a party with the addition of their mothers, but Lettie didn't mind as much as she knew she should. It was nice to have everyone in the apartment that had always meant so much to her, working to help her. "So, what did you learn, Mom?"

"Not too much, but I got his number, so now I can check in without suspicion. He doesn't plan to stay here permanently, but said he's been looking into smaller magical hubs for a while now. He went on and on about how the big cities with magic are already developed, but places like this have a lot of untapped potential, that they cater to a more rural crowd or city folks wanting to get away. Didn't quite seem to see the irony in him wanting to modernize a place he's trying to lure us poor, empty-headed country folk to."

"So, what's the plan? Do we actually use magic on him or just…Hey, Chandler," Amelia popped up from her window seat. "How litigious is he? Because I bet the two of us could really freak him out."

"Oh, he'll sue in a heartbeat, but there's not really a case if he can't prove we're doing anything. He can't sue us because he's scared of magic. And he knows it because one of his first purchases was next to a shifter couple. He was terrified of the kid. They were little, could barely control their powers. He tried to get them evicted."

"What an asshole. Here you go. Who wants a drink?" Ginger said, handing a cup to Monica.

"No one else drinks that shit, mom." Chandler scrunched her nose.

"Give it here. I'll make it palatable." Amelia stretched out her hand for the mixer and glanced at Lettie. "Okay if I raid?"

"Raid away." Lettie waved her hand in permission. "So, for the official business of the Lilac Lake Lifesavers—" Lorne booed the name and Lettie flipped him off. "How do we start this?"

"Invite him to the bar," Amelia said, smashing cherries in a cup. "It's the off season so all the patrons are locals. He'll feel compelled to see it since it's the closest drinking spot to the Lodge, and he'll hate it because even humans say they can feel the magic in there."

"And then you compel him to drown himself in the lake?" Lorne swiped the tequila off the counter and poured it directly down his throat.

"No, I was thinking of starting somewhere other than homicide." Amelia said. "I think Daphne has the least usable skills."

"Hey!" Daphne looked up from the magazine she had started to read while the rest of them argued. "If the going gets bad, I get screaming."

"That's my girl." Lorne handed the bottle of tequila to her.

"Personally," Monica said, sipping her aggressively neon green drink. "I think you're all overthinking. It's scaring a two-hundred-dollar haircut in a suit, not brain surgery. How tough can he be?"

Amelia and Daphne began arguing, Lorne yelled something, and the happiness Lettie had felt suddenly drained away, replaced by panic. This wasn't a funny game or a garden party. None of this should be happening. She should be focused on updating the inn, planning the festival with Amelia, and honoring her grandmother's legacy.

Instead, it was the same circular conversation without a true goal, without a plan. Just making Alvin afraid of their magic and hoping it was enough to get out of a contract. And even if they pulled that off, she still had to figure out the rest of her life—how to run a hotel in the peak season, how to be a girlfriend, how to trust Chander. And she couldn't plan for any of it because she was stuck cleaning up a mess she hadn't made. Her heart was a thunderous thing, pounding as if it wanted to escape her chest.

"Jesus, this is impossible." Lettie yelled and looked at her hands, surprised to find them coated in a web of green magic. Everyone was silent, staring at her. She waved her hands, and the tv turned on. The lights flickered. "Oh, god. Sorry, I just—"

"Sweetheart, are you using magic?" Monica took a tentative step towards her.

"She sure as shit is," Chandler said, rushing around the counter. "She's been doing great!" She paused. "Sorry, big mouth."

"It's okay." Lettie tried to cross her arms, but Lorne caught her by the wrist.

"This is good, Lettie. This is real good. It means you're feeling something. Powerful magic is powerful emotion. You don't have to bottle everything up all the time."

"I don't want to talk about this," Lettie said, feeling her cheeks heat. She'd invited everyone she knew to her house to watch her have a meltdown. The air seemed thin, and her magic flashed like fireworks.

"Shit, girl. Have a drink. A little wayward magic is nothing to get worked up over. We've all done it. Haven't all blown up town square, but believe me, we've all had our magic do things we don't want." Amelia handed her a glass with a drink that looked much more appetizing than Monica's.

Daphne put her magazine back on the coffee table. "See, that's what I've been telling you. We love you, Letts. You're allowed to have a little breakdown. We know you're not seventeen anymore."

There was a weight Lettie carried with her, a fear that her magic, like much of the magic that came from Lilac Lake, was dangerous. That if she didn't hold it tight, she would hurt someone. The belief had become so ingrained over the years that at some point she had stopped questioning it, just believed it to be true.

But the explosion had happened when she was a teenager, when her life was volatile, when she was so scared of losing Chandler that the dial on every emotion was turned up to a hundred.

She realized her jaw was clenched and loosened her muscles. Everyone was looking at her as if she was in the spotlight. "I have always been so scared to hurt someone," she whispered.

Ginger was the first to speak, "Honey, we're all a little scared of our magic, but it's a gift. It's only dangerous if you need it to be. Look at the rest of us, named for monsters from legends. The world wants us to be afraid because we have power. Don't let them take that from you because you were a kid once."

"But people are scared. That's what we're doing, isn't it? We're using this man's fear against him. What if they're right?" She played with the hem of her shirt, unable to make eye contact with anyone.

"Shit, Lettie," Lorne said. "I had no idea you worried about that. I wish I had known. That man is scared of his own prejudice. And if he's really that scared of people like us, why's he doing business with us? Why's he trying to make money off our town if he thinks we're dangerous? We deserve places to live where people like him aren't, because we're never going to get the world, as shit as that is. So, we got our towns and our communities, and we're allowed to fight for them. And he knows it."

Monica blinked. "Baby, that's…you're absolutely right."

"Well, don't look too shocked or you're gonna hurt my feelings."

Ginger glanced at her daughter, but Lettie could not read the thoughts clouding her eyes. "I apologize if I'm speaking out of turn, but Chandler was a mess when she first got here. She was angry and sad and…"

"Broken," Chandler said.

"And he knew it. He'd worked with her. Gwen knew it. They knew they were taking advantage. And maybe it's not right, I'm sure a lot of people would say 'a deals a deal.' But I think if you go around treating people wrong you can't be too upset if you get mistreated yourself."

"I'm sorry, but I'm simply not going to spend my time crying because some sleazy dude didn't get to take advantage of someone. This is my home. I like it the way it is. And yeah, I'm mad at Chandler too, but I'd be fighting this even if she didn't want the lodge," Amelia said. "You know damn well that's not what your grandmothers wanted when they wrote their wills. And I'm not going to watch one of my favorite places get turned into a soulless boutique hotel because our town lawyer can't write decent contracts."

"Okay, okay." Lettie nodded. But she had another fear, one that was in direct opposition to her worries. "What if it doesn't work? What if he won't sign it over?"

"Then I'm going to lose money, I already told you that. It'll wipe out my savings, but I'm staying. I'm not going anywhere," Chandler said.

"Don't worry about that," Lorne said, grabbing shot glasses from Lettie's top cabinet. They were hand painted, beautiful things her grandmother had collected. "Because if he doesn't want to back out, he's going to find Lilac Lake real inhospitable, and not in the way y'all are planning, but in the way where I'm going to drive his ass right out of town."

"Lorne…" Monica took a shot.

"What?" He downed his own. "That's my sister, and this is my Gran's place. I'm not just relying on all you spooky women—though I'm sure you'll all do great."

Chandler pulled Lettie aside, dragging her into the sitting room and away from the others. "I think you're incredible." She kissed Lettie softly. "But I know what it's like to fear your magic. We'll work through it together, okay? I'm here. I promise, I'm here to stay."

Lettie ran her thumb over Chandler's cheek and then traced her lips. She'd let Chandler go long ago, but she'd still shown up in her dreams, haunted her memories. Having her back was possibly the most frightening thing of all, because now she was no teenager, this was no first love, hot and heavy and fleeting. "Every day I worry I'll wake up and you'll be gone."

"I know. And every day I think about it, but I choose you. I choose to stay. I am a runner, Lettie, but I'm tired of it. I'm not here out of obligation or guilt. I'm here because this is my home, because there are things here—people here—worth fighting for, even if I'm fighting myself."

"What if you change your mind?" The words sounded childish, even to Lettie, but the fear was there. Was she giving her heart to someone who was only going to toss it aside?

"I can't tell the future, but for the first time in a long time I want something that doesn't make me feel bad. You, this Lodge, upholding a family legacy, it's something I'm proud of." Chandler took her hand and intertwined their fingers. "I've done very little I'm proud of, when I look back on my life I'm mostly ashamed, and I'm so tired of feeling that way. I want this. I want something good and real. I want you." She brought Lettie's hand to her mouth and kissed her knuckles.

Lettie pulled her hand free and wrapped her arms around Chandler, pulling her close. She kissed her, reveling in the taste of her, in the dark magic that lurked beneath her skin. "Okay. If you say we're in it together, I'll trust you."

"We are." Chandler kissed her again. "I'm here. I'm staying."

-CHAPTER TWENTY-ONE-

MAYBE SHE WAS being foolish, but Chandler's promise to stay felt like a shield against all the other bullshit Lettie had on her plate. She'd spent very few nights in her own apartment, instead finding her way to Chandler's apartment and into her bed.

Slats of moonlight illuminated the sharp features of the gorgon's face, and her eyes blazed each time she looked down on Lettie, whispering dirty things into the darkness that made Lettie's heart race.

"You are mine," she said, her lips against Lettie's skin, her fingers buried inside her.

Lettie barely had the thoughts to respond, lost in the feeling of Chandler the building orgasm blooming in her core. Her magic danced around her as she came, filling the room with green light.

The gorgon within Chandler flashed, her eyes slit like a snake's, her skin stone gray, and she lowered her mouth to Lettie's breast, her fingers coaxing the last of her orgasm out of her.

She was human again when she lifted her head, her face flushed. "You are mine," she repeated, lowering herself to the bed. She trailed her fingers over Lettie's abdomen. "My powerful witch."

"Are you mine?" Lettie asked, pressing her lips to Chandler's collarbone and tasting the sweat-salted skin.

"Yes," Chandler said. "For as long as you will have me."

Forever. She almost said the word, could feel it heavy in her throat, but she swallowed it down. There were other words tangled with it, ones she had not acknowledged, even to herself. "Us," she finally said. "I think I was always waiting for this."

"Me too." Chandler continued the trail of her fingers, raising goosebumps on Lettie's flesh. "I didn't even admit it to myself, but I knew. I knew if I saw you again…" Her voice trailed away, and she cleared her throat. "I'm going to get it right this time."

Despite herself, Lettie believed her. "Let me see your magic," she said, holding up her hand. "What he's so scared of."

"You sure?"

"Yeah. Call it a sick curiosity." She flexed her fingers, watching the tendons move, the creases at her knuckles.

"Okay," Chandler's voice was breathless. Her tongue darted out, wetting her bottom lip and her eyes fluttered closed.

Lettie's hand was stone.

Her heart pounded, but there was no pain, just a strange numbness and the heaviness of the stone at the end of her wrist. Then it was gone, her skin returned. "Whoa. That's incredible."

"I guess." Chandler sighed. "I've always been jealous of witches. That's real magic. I can't even use mine." The snakes inked across her body seemed to move in the moonlight as she turned on her side. "Your turn."

Lettie closed her eyes, imagining her magic as a pool contained within her, deep and clear. Wind whipped across her skin and when she opened her eyes the room was bathed in warm green light.

"How could you ever doubt this was good?" Chandler moved, straddling Lettie, naked and gorgeous. She cupped Lettie's breasts and threw her head back, the green light painting her dark hair. "I can feel *you* in it." She pressed her slick core against Lettie. "And you feel amazing."

Lettie slipped a hand between them, brushing her fingers against Chandler's clit and letting her magic escape freely. But it was Chandler who got herself off, writhing and drunk on Lettie's magic.

"More," she said, reaching down and guiding Lettie's fingers inside her. She increased her speed, arching her back, her breasts illuminated in green magic, nipples peaked.

Lettie watched her as she came, the way her neck curved, her mouth round and full, Lettie's name on her lips. She clenched around Lettie and then collapsed forward against her chest.

Lettie brushed her fingers over Chandler's hair. *Hers.* She urged Chandler's head up until she was looking at her. "Mine," she said, capturing Chandler's mouth with her own.

The gorgon wrapped Lettie in her arms, digging her fingers into her hair. She pulled Lettie's lip between her teeth, biting so hard Lettie gasped, and then she released her. "Let's stay like this all day."

Lettie thought she would like that, surrounded by magic and darkness, tangled with Chandler, coaxing orgasms out of each other, separated from the world. "That would be nice."

But she knew the world was out there waiting, and tomorrow they would face it.

Lettie supposed if Alvin was a completely different man, he wouldn't be so bad, he was a little funny and always listened when she talked.

Unfortunately, she knew his listening skills came from his desire to scam her. Though he praised her knowledge of the town, he'd brought up her perceived lack of hotel experience several times, suggesting his own list of hotel managers, only smiling when she pointed out Pepper already had the job.

She nodded along, playing dumb and laughing at his jokes, but she'd drink the entire lake before she let him swindle The Stone and Sorcery Lodge away from her.

Lettie drummed her fingers on the coffee shop table, letting magic spark with each tap. "Listen, you and I both know Chandler wants out of this deal."

His gaze flicked to her fingers and back towards her face. "Chandler approached us. She was clearly upset. I was doing her a favor." A muscle in his jaw twitched.

"Were you? A clearly distraught former employee contacted her ex-girlfriend. Was the call even about the Lodge or did you see an opportunity and exploit it?" Fuck this man and fuck being subtle. If she had to listen to him mansplain her own town to her one more time, she was going to strangle him.

He scooted his chair closer to the table. "Lettie, a valued former employee called a colleague wanting out of her hometown. Let's not dwell on this. You and I could have a valuable partnership."

Another tap. Another spark of magic. "And how long after signing did she ask to back out of the contract, Mr. Condon?"

He cleared his throat. "Two days."

"So, within two days she regretted selling her *grandmother's* legacy. The ink was barely dry. Is this generally how you do business?" She hoped next time he got his oat milk latte it burned the roof of his mouth clean off.

"Holding people to contract? Yes, it is. She knows how to get out of it. This is the first I'm hearing of your trepidation. Frankly, I think it is unfair to blame me."

"I blame her as well. She's a grown woman, and she shouldn't have entered a contract out of anger. But is the money really going to matter to you? It's a couple thousand dollars, your suit probably costs about half of that. But the thing is, Mr. Condon, the more I talk with you, the less I want to do business with you. I don't think you understand this town or *my* vision for *my* Lodge. I certainly signed nothing, nor would I. So, why don't we settle this together?" This time she let her magic flare, shooting sparks towards the ceiling.

For a moment he was silent, running his tongue over his teeth. "What are you suggesting?"

Should she play nice? Her mother certainly thought so. But Lettie was so tired of being nice. "You should void the contract, Mr. Condon.

Void the contract and find another town to bother. Lilac Lake isn't interested in your kind of progress."

The muscle in his jaw twitched harder. He templed his fingers together. "Ms. Katz, did you know you own the only commercial land on the lake?"

"Yes."

He chuckled, but it was humorless. "Of course you did. You're a smart girl. But it's not the *only* land on the lake. Do you trust the entire city government? Do you think there are no palms that can be greased? And do you think you could compete with a real hotel? Not that rinky-dink shack some backwoods in your family no doubt built, but something shiny and new?"

"Why do you even want to be here? You clearly don't care for supernaturals, so why are you so interested in this town?"

"Personally, I'm not, but my bosses are. Regular folks aren't interested in the magic of the cities anymore. It's mundane. Most supernaturals have integrated, they're everywhere. But places like this, places with a hint of danger, they still hold intrigue. And this is a gorgeous town, with the right developments the lake could be a tourist attraction on its own. I've seen pictures of this place in spring. My company has a hotel in every major city in the United States, we're expanding internationally, but these are our untapped markets. And you, simply, cannot compete."

She wrapped her hands around the cup of tea in front of her and the contents bubbled, splashing out of the cup and onto the table. "I think you'd be surprised what I can do, Alvin." And though she hadn't meant to do it, the glass cracked and popped. Liquid seeped across the table, reflecting Lettie's magic like a mirror.

Alvin jumped up as Margery came rushing forward from behind the counter. "Lettie! Are you okay?"

"Sorry about that, Margery." She glanced around the coffee shop.

"Oh, it's no problem." She flicked her fingers towards the spill, rounding up the liquid into a neat puddle in the center of the table. "Just spooked me." She looked over at Alvin. "You look like you've seen a ghost. Its just a little magic, hun. You know our Lettie here is a real powerful witch. Blew up the town square once." She looked back at Lettie and winked before mopping up the mess with a dishrag. "Lots of powerful folk around here." She smiled before heading back towards the front of the shop.

"Is that really how you want to play this? Threatening me?"

"I'm not threatening you. I'm informing you I have no interest in working with you, that this town has no interest in your business."

"Is that why you sent your mother? She's a simple woman, Ms. Katz, easy on the eyes but rather transparent, asking about my plans, my business. Why would she care?"

Had she overplayed her hand? But it was going to come to this eventually—threatening the man, making him terrified of their magic— what other end could there be? She stood up and pushed her chair in. "I simply think you should reevaluate your contract. No one has to lose money on this. I'll be at The Three Sisters tonight. Why don't you think it over and then we'll have a drink, talk this through like adults."

"I'm very disappointed, Ms. Katz. I thought we could work well together. But you must think I'm an idiot if you believe I'll go to a siren's bar when I'm already being manipulated."

Lettie laughed. "I don't think Amelia would appreciate your insinuations. Mind control is illegal. I'm only asking you to meet me at the closest bar."

"Why don't *you* think it over? Think about the money you'll make. Chandler is…she's flighty. I'm sure she has your heart all aflutter, but we're talking about your future, about true wealth. I'm going to do my best to forget this conversation, we all have off days where our frustration gets the best of us. I'm also going to move forward with my departure, after all, I don't own this place for another few months. I can wait it out."

-CHAPTER TWENTY-TWO-

"SO, YOU DECIDED against subtlety, huh?" Chandler raised her voice to be heard over the noise in The Three Sisters. Veins of stone crackled down the side of her glass as she ran her finger around the rim.

"I asked myself, 'what would Chandler do' and, yeah, I got a little threatening." Lettie grabbed Chandler's whiskey and poured it down her throat. A few hours removed from the situation, she was feeling less sure of her decision.

"Interesting technique from the woman who was feeling guilty about the whole thing a few days ago." Chandler smirked.

"Hey." Oak slid into the seat beside her, followed by Daphne with a tray full of drinks. "I heard you had a whole secret meeting without me."

"You're too sweet to be threatening, Oakey" Chandler said, ruffling their hair and earning a shove to her shoulder.

"Is that true?" Daphne handed them a drink. "Do you shift into, like, a bunny?"

"Yeah," They looked Daphne over. "Wanna see?"

"Another time, definitely. So how did the meeting go today?"

Lettie sighed. "Well, that depends on how you feel about subtle threats of violence."

"Personally, I'm pro," Daphne said. "Why make him think we *might* hurt him when we can make him cower wondering when we're *going* to hurt him."

Oak rubbed their temples with their pointer fingers. "What I'm hearing is you're all going to need a bail fund."

"No way. He's not going to go to the police. 'Outsider steals family Lodge from local woman' is not a good headline. His firm will want him to deal with this diplomatically," Chandler said, with a curious twinkle in her eye.

"He threatened to build a hotel to compete with ours if I don't cooperate. Said he can get the mayor in his pocket."

Oak scoffed. "Good luck with that. There's an election coming up, I doubt Molina is going to want to stir anything up, and a big hotel right on the lake would definitely do that."

"I wouldn't count on that," Daphne said, swirling the straw in her drink. "Molina's an idiot. He only wins because no one runs against him."

"Maybe someone should run against him," Chandler said, glancing around at the others. "What? Not me, obviously. But someone."

The door to the bar flew open, banging into the wall. The room fell silent, so dramatically Lettie almost laughed until she saw Alvin Condon standing in the frame. Though he was still in a suit, his hair was disheveled, or at least disheveled compared to how he usually looked. His gaze caught on Lettie.

Chandler chucked as noise returned to the bar and scooted her chair out, angling her body towards Lettie. "What's up, Alvin." She grinned, adjusting her septum ring.

Daphne gazed up at him, fluttering her lashes and throwing her long hair over her shoulder. "Oh no, you look mad."

Across the bar, Lettie saw Amelia freeze in the middle of making a drink, her eyes on the situation unfolding as Alvin placed his palms flat on the table. "Lettie, Chandler, I'd like to speak with you."

"Speak then," Daphne said, leaning back in her seat. "And watch your mitts, you're able to spill my drink."

"Privately," he said, but his eyes stayed on Daphne.

"No," Chandler said. "But you're free to take a seat." She kicked the chair across from her out from under the table.

That same muscle as before twitched in his jaw. Lettie wondered if he could feel it moving under his skin. She watched the silent battle between Alvin and Chandler, and in the end, he sat, looking about as uncomfortable as she'd ever seen a person look.

"Well, what's up?" Lettie asked, trying to keep her voice calm and casual.

"I just received a call from my boss that your local newspaper reached out for comment on me stealing the Lodge from Everly Hart's granddaughter."

'Outsider steals local Lodge' indeed.

Smirking, Chandler drummed her fingers against the table, turning it to stone. The veins of rock inched closer to Alvin with each beat of her fingers. "Oh, and what did you say?"

"I'm so glad I fired you—"

"That's a weird thing to say to a newspaper," Oak interrupted, earning a chuckle from Daphne.

"Fuck all of you. You signed a contract, Chandler! I'm not in the business of coddling unhinged women. I'm not your therapist. So all this act—like I'm the bad guy for buying something from you when you were upset—isn't going to work on me. You want out, send a check." The tip of Alvin's nose had turned red.

"Pay me my severance." Chandler's fingers continued to tap, and the stone continued its journey across the table.

"You don't get severance for gross misconduct. Did you tell your little girlfriend about that? How you showed up to the office drunk and crying? Does she know you're a fucking mess?"

Now it was Chandler's turn to blush.

"I think that's enough," Daphne said, her voice sharp and biting. She downed the rest of her drink and raised the glass above her head, signaling to Amelia.

"Oh, and what kind of monster is threatening me now?" He pulled his hands from the table as the stone brushed against his fingers.

"Banshee, baby." Daphne started to hum under her breath, nothing truly threatening, but the tune raised the hairs on Lettie's arms.

The red flush spread further across Alvin's face, making him look like he might explode. "I told James there wasn't much in this town, but I was wrong. It's *beautiful*. So much untouched land. Cheap land, too. I was going to leave soon, but maybe I'll stay."

"I don't think you will," Amelia said, bringing over their drink order. "In fact, I'd like you to leave."

"I'll leave when I'm done." He reached for one of the drinks and curled his fingers around the glass, but before he could bring it to his lips Amelia leaned over the table.

Her voice was as sweet as honey, dripping from her lips. "Stand up."

Though Alvin's eyes went wide, he complied, standing on wobbly legs.

Amelia put her hand on his shoulder. "You're going to walk to the door. You're going to leave my bar and you aren't going to return tonight. Right?"

"Right," he said, but his mouth struggled against the words, even as they spilled out of him, and his legs jerked like a toy soldier's as he left the bar. No one at the table spoke until the door shut behind him.

Amelia wiped her hands on her jeans and sighed. "Asshole."

"Can you…," Oak said, then apparently thinking better of it, clamped their mouth shut.

"I try not to, but it's all above board if he's posing a threat." She slipped into the seat he had vacated. "So first, can you please restore my table to its sticky glory?"

Chandler tapped her fingers on the table, and it returned to wood. "My apologies."

"Secondly, he seemed more pissed than afraid."

Daphne picked up her drink, "Yeah. Maybe overplayed things a bit. What can I say, we're not used to being villains. Though I think that leaves us, like, one option left. Scare the shit out of him."

"Normally not my style, but I don't care for that man. I'm in," Oak said, running a hand through their curls.

"Okay, sure, but…" Lettie had a few reservations about this plan and her stomach felt like she'd eaten a handful of gravel. While she believed in her friends' ability to terrorize a man, he had more money than they did. And she knew, whatever the world said about magic, money was power.

Chandler reached under the table and squeezed Lettie's knee, helping to calm her nerves. Then her fingers strayed higher, rubbing a circle on Lettie's thigh and filling her with an entirely different emotion. "You're worried about the town?"

"He's right. We can't compete with him if he opens a hotel on the lake. We wanted to scare him away, not create an enemy," Lettie said.

Amelia scooted Lettie's drink across the table, and she downed it. This was her fault. They had a plan, albeit not a very good one, but she'd lost her temper and now he was going to put the Lodge out of business.

"Okay." Chandler nodded. "I can pay him the money. It's most of what I have, but I'll be fine. The Lodge makes enough." She stood up.

And Lettie grabbed her arm, pulling her back down. "No. I don't want that."

"One of us could run for mayor," Oak offered, their eyes beginning to grow glassy with intoxication. "Or city council or something. Really make him work for it."

Daphne rested her chin on her hand, looking at Oak. "You could run for mayor. You'd look good on those little signs."

Oak blushed, and Chandler cleared her throat. "Let's table that discussion until everyone is a little more sober."

But Daphne turned her attention to Amelia, twirling a strand of hair around her finger. "Could you make him do it? It could be like a little secret."

"Oh, yeah. And I'm sure I'd look good in an orange jumpsuit. No, I can't make him do it.

"Fine." She pretended to pout. "Break my heart."

"I know you said to stop apologizing, but I really am so sorry I put you in this position," Chandler said after they left the bar.

Lettie tugged her jacket tighter. The night was overcast, leaving the streets dark except for the pools of yellow light under the streetlamps, spaced too far apart to do much good. "Were you really such a mess when you first got here?"

The image of it didn't really fit in with the Chandler she knew. She seemed so sure of herself, leather and tattoos and a strong jaw that never seemed to quiver.

Now, she didn't look quite so strong. "It felt like the last straw when she broke up with me. Like, I'd never managed to get my life together the way other people had, but she had it all figured out. So I thought if I had her maybe I'd have it together too. And then I got fired because I was awful at my job, and she broke up with me, and I just…I fell apart. Then I came here and you…you'd grown up. And I didn't think I could do it. I didn't think I could see you every day, and you'd be beautiful and wonderful and funny, and I'd be a fucking disaster. So, I got drunk, and I called her and…"

"I don't have it all figured out either." Between the streetlamps, cloaked in darkness, Lettie stepped closer, tracing Chandler's face with her eyes.

Chandler's gaze flicked to Lettie's mouth, and she kissed her urgently, harshly. Her fingers twined through Lettie's hair, tugging at the roots.

There were no more words to say. And even with the danger of Alvin Condon hanging over them, Lettie was more complete than she had been in a long time, a puzzle with the last piece finally put into place.

There was no losing herself in Chandler, instead she had found something, her magic, her desire. All the things she had let slip away over the years.

And she realized she had just been going through the motions for years. She deepened their kiss, sweeping her tongue through Chandler's mouth, the earthy, spiced taste of her sweet on Lettie's tongue. Every day Lettie had gotten up, gone to work, done all the things she was supposed to do.

Now she was doing nothing she was supposed to do. She was threatening men in bars and making scenes. She was blackmailing and—Lettie realized with a start—she was falling in love.

Falling for a mess of a woman with curly hair and sinister magic that snaked through Lettie's veins. Falling into something that she couldn't see the end of, didn't know where it would go or how things would work. And for the first time in a long time, that didn't scare her. She didn't need to know the ending. She just needed now. These moments, this woman.

Somehow, she knew, she would figure the rest of it out.

-CHAPTER TWENTY-THREE-

IN THE LIGHT of day, with Chandler quietly humming as she typed on her laptop, the whole incident with Alvin didn't seem *quite* as bad.

Thinking about him staying in town, buying votes she was sure were for sale, still made her stomach hurt. But she tried not to think about him and instead focused on what she could control—The Stone and Sorcery Lodge. Renovations were going great, the cabins were on schedule for the most part, and however things ended up playing out, it would be hers. Hers and Chandler's.

For now, that had to be enough. And, mostly, it was. Every time she looked at the cabins, the fresh paint, and the full guest list she felt the satisfaction of a dream fulfilled. All she had to do was hold on to it, and maybe this time things would work out. She had to believe that.

Someone knocked on the door to her apartment, and Daphne jumped up from the couch. "Coming!" She pulled the door open to reveal a very hungover Oak rubbing their eyes.

"Good morning, my little ray of sunshine." Daphne ushered them inside. "Coffee? Advil?"

"Both." Oak sank into the couch cushions.

"Look at you. Old age is catching up. You used to drink me under the table," Chandler teased.

"I can still drink you under the table." Oak glared. "That guy is worse than I imagined when you used to call me complaining about him. Please tell me y'all have come up with some brilliant plan."

"I'm going to speak with that reporter today. Shame him locally. If he really plans to buy up land, I want to get ahead of the story."

There was another knock on the door, and they all looked at each other before Lettie got up and answered it. Pepper was standing in the doorway, looking frazzled.

"Hey, can you come out to the lobby? I need backup."

Lettie looked down at her clothes. She was still in her pajamas. But the look on Pepper's face told her she didn't have time to change. She glanced over her shoulder at the others, then slipped into the hallway. "What's going on?"

"Oh, you'll see." Pepper rushed down the hallway, her long hair swaying behind her.

Raised voices came through the walls before Lettie made it to the lobby, and she braced herself because she recognized both of them. Herschel was standing only inches from Alvin Condon, outrage clear on his face and in the way he pointed his finger in the younger man's face.

What was he even doing here? She looked to Pepper who must have read the question on her face.

"He likes to read the paper here sometimes. Says it's more peaceful than the diner. Apparently, he wasn't feeling very peaceful today."

"I don't even know who you are, old man," Alvin said, his back ramrod straight.

"Exactly! Everyone knows you don't belong here. We all know you were yelling at Lettie last night, and my granddaughter is going to publish it in the paper. You've got no business here, and you certainly have no business telling Pepper how to do her job."

Lettie glanced at Pepper again.

"He said I need to dress more professionally."

Oh, hell no. Lettie squeezed Pepper's arm, then walked towards the two men, steeling herself. "Hey, Herschel."

The anger evaporated from his face at her voice. "Did Chandler really sign the Lodge over to this weasel?"

"We're working on it. Some men don't have the same morals as we have here."

"Oh, that's rich," Alvin said. "I suppose you'd pass up a good business deal just because some woman was sniveling when she signed the papers."

The rage returned to Herschel. "You bet your ass I would."

"As if you've ever had the opportunity. What do you have? Crying waitresses?"

"Enough." Truly, Lettie had had enough. "Mr. Condon, am I to understand you're criticizing my employee's attire? "

"She's wearing a t-shirt." He gestured at Pepper, who was, in fact, wearing a t-shirt under her blazer. Alvin closed his eyes and breathed deeply. "There's a level of professionalism…"

"And you believe *you* possess that?" Lettie asked.

"Yes! Generally, yes. But this town is like…you people are infuriating!"

Lettie halfway believed him. There was no way he went around screaming at everyone all the time and, for a second, just a second, she had a spasm of sympathy course through her. He'd had no idea what he was walking into. "Well," she said, "as you know, whatever the outcome of our disagreement, you have no ownership of this place for a few months still. So, you'll keep your comments on my employees to yourself, or I'm afraid you won't be welcome here. Understood?"

"As if I'm welcome now." He made the smallest movement towards Lettie and Herschel moved in between them.

"Son, I think it's best you get going. There's a lot of towns across this country. Perhaps you'll find one of them better suited to you than this one."

"Walk with me," Lettie said, "And please forgive my unprofessional attire. I was not expecting you this morning. I'll see you later, Herschel. It's okay. I promise." She turned and headed for the front door.

Outside the wind was blowing, and she wished she had a jacket. "Why are you here?" she asked as soon as they were out of earshot of any guests.

"I came to apologize for last night. There is no reason for us to be screaming at each other. I meant what I said, this is not my usual demeanor."

Though she knew he didn't go around screaming at everyone, she had a hunch he was always this overbearing and rude. It might not be what he presented to the world, but underneath the neat, professional show he put on, she suspected he was an angry, scared man. She was sure he wasn't kind to his employees. "And yet you caused another scene in my Lodge. It isn't even noon yet, Mr. Condon."

She was sick of this man who seemed to have oozed into every aspect of her life, her home, her job, her favorite bar, her girlfriend. She stopped walking and turned to stare at him, wondering what more he could have to say for himself.

He seemed to struggle for control over himself as he chose his words. "Lettie, I am sure Chandler is a lot of fun. I've seen her brand of fun after hours many times, in many clubs. You're, no doubt, having a blast. But we both know the moment you get on board with me she'll leave. And I *will* have a hotel here. You're giving up a lot of money if you keep on this way."

Boring. She'd already heard this speech. "Maybe Chandler would run, but she's not running right now, is she? She's here. Either way, I don't care. I don't want your money. We have, like, five businesses in Lilac Lake. Where would I spend all that money? It's freezing, Alvin, and I'm tired of this conversation. Consider what you saw last night the real me."

He smiled. "But it's not. That's a mask. You're a good girl."

Magic sparked at her fingertips, warming her. The ground beneath her feet shook, just as it had years ago, and visions of that day filled her mind: Chandler, her face pinched, tears streaming down her cheeks, Lettie begging her to stay.

Another rumble.

Chandler, grasping Lettie's hands, trying to explain so much, too young to have the words to express everything she felt as the ground shook and turned to stone beneath them. Lettie had kissed her then, desperate and pleading, and everything had happened so fast she could barely recall anything except being broken apart and left standing in a pile of rubble.

And Chandler had run, only glancing back once, crying harder than before, leaving Lettie. Then the police sirens, and the people, and the ambulance even though she wasn't hurt. There wasn't a scratch on her, but her heart had been broken.

She cleared her mind and looked into Alvin's eyes. There was fear, true fear, as the ground shook beneath him. "Don't come back to my Lodge. Go back to wherever you're staying. Call your lawyer, tell him you're voiding the contract. I don't want to see you again." The ground stilled.

He straightened his tie. "Happily, as soon as Chandler sends me the eight thousand dollars she owes me."

Rage built inside Lettie, too much for the situation. She knew it, knew she should get control of herself. But all she could think of was Chandler running, the way she had wanted more, and the world had never given it to her. The way even Lettie had struggled to find her place. How hard things were for no reason except men like this, happy to take and take and never give.

She was cold, and she was tired. She was…strong. She deserved The Stone and Sorcery Lodge. She deserved love and happiness and a life free of all this bullshit that never seemed to end. She was mad at Chandler. Mad at her grandmother for never telling her this plan. Mad at Hillchamp for being a terrible lawyer.

Her magic grew, a green orb in her hand, bathing them in sickly light on the overcast day. She watched as it grew, filled with curiosity.

"Lettie!" Daphne's arm clamped around her wrist and the magic snuffed out like a candle. Daphne looked into her eyes. "Not like this."

"Oh, Jesus Christ," Alvin said. "I knew this was going to be too much effort. I told Gwen we should just buy land on the lake. But no, I let her talk me into this. But I was right, that there's nothing like a lesbian who thinks she's in love to do some crazy—"

Daphne's fist connected with his face. Her eyes were wide, and she stared at her hand. "Shit. Fuck. My bad." She reached for Lettie again and ran, dragging Lettie with her.

"What just happened?" Lettie asked, glancing behind her at Alvin who still had his hand on his face. "Holy shit. Oh, God Daphne, you hit him."

When they were around the side of Lodge, Daphne stopped running and put her hands on her knees. "I did. I hit him. I didn't mean to. I was going to stop you from zapping him with your magic and then he opened his mouth."

"And you shut it." Lettie knew she shouldn't be laughing. Daphne had just assaulted a man, but she couldn't help herself. She started to laugh and then she couldn't stop even as tears rolled down her cheeks. "He's a punchable man."

"I don't punch people!" Daphne paced back and forth, running her hands through her hair. Her voice was at an uncomfortable pitch, and it echoed through Lettie's head. "I should go apologize."

"No. No!" Lettie grasped for her, pulling her back. "I don't think you should. Maybe like a text or something?

"A text!" Daphne was shrill and birds scattered out of the trees nearby, squawking their displeasure.

"Daph, pitch. My eardrums are going to explode."

"Sorry," she whispered and covered her mouth with her hand. "He's going to call the cops. I'm going to get arrested."

Lettie grabbed her shoulders. "You aren't going to get arrested." *Hopefully.* She didn't add that. "Come on. Let's go inside."

They went in through a backdoor, avoiding guests. Lettie led Daphne toward their apartment, trying not to let the uncertainty she was feeling show on her face. What the fuck were they going to do? He definitely wouldn't sign anything now.

Chandler was going to have to eat that money. Lettie didn't see any other solution. Would she really do it? Had she changed enough to stick around when things got tough? Lettie wanted to believe she had, but there was a small part of her that still doubted Chandler and worried one day she'd wake up and Chandler would be gone.

Oak was laughing in the living room when Lettie and Daphne walked in, but it died on their lips, and they jumped up from their seat. "What happened?"

Daphne held her hands up, staring at them like wild badgers were attached to the ends of her arms. "Fuck."

Chandler looked to Lettie, putting down the coffee she had been sipping. "Lettie, what happened? Daphne looks like she's about to pass out."

"She punched Alvin."

Chandler snorted. "Oh shit, really?"

"Yes," Daphne wailed, and her hand shot to her mouth. "I don't want to go to jail. He was just—He was saying some awful, homophobic shit."

"He's not going to have you arrested," Chandler said. She walked to Daphne and looked into her eyes. "He's already floundering here. He isn't going to call the police and get them involved while I'm talking to a journalist. Just…leave him alone for now." Chandler pried Daphne's hands from her face. "Daphne, it's going to be okay."

Lettie watched Chandler, the gentle movement of her hands as she led Daphne to the couch and rubbed circles on her back. Lettie had never thought this moment would happen—kindness passing between Daphne and Chandler, who had spent their entire childhoods arguing. But there Chandler was, talking Daphne down from a panic attack.

She wanted to pull Chandler up, drag her to her room, bury her face between her thighs—which was definitely not the right emotion for the moment. But that simple action, consoling Lettie's friend, had soothed the confusion she had felt and this time she thought it might be permanent.

She'd spent the last few weeks going back and forth in her mind. Half of her trusting Chandler, the other half waiting for her to bolt. Not once when they'd been together as teenagers had she said a kind word to Daphne. Not once had she tried.

But they weren't teenagers anymore. They were grown women. Life had done a real number on Chandler, but she'd come out on the other side and she'd come back. Now, despite the futility—and if Lettie was being honest, stupidity—of their plan Chandler was fighting. Fighting for the Lodge and Lilac Lake. Fighting for this life they could build together. Fighting for Lettie.

-CHAPTER TWENTY-FOUR-

THAT NIGHT, ONCE Daphne had finally fallen asleep, Lettie snuck across the hallway. She was sure Chandler would still be awake, so she didn't knock, taking her chances with the knob. It turned and Lettie slipped inside.

Blue light from the television filled the apartment. Chandler looked up from where she was lying on the couch. "Hey, beautiful."

Lettie pulled her shirt over her head and wiggled out of her pants before sliding onto the couch with Chandler. She rested her head on Chandler's chest, listening to the beat of her heart. "How did your interview go?"

"Surprisingly good, actually." Chandler pressed her nose to Lettie's hair and inhaled.

"I forgive you," Lettie said, trying to glance up at her, but she couldn't see Chandler's face and she was glad for it. "For the contract. For everything. I know I already said I did, and I mostly meant it, or at least I wanted to mean it, but now I do."

"I love you, Lettie," Chandler said.

Lettie could feel her flinch when she went stiff in her arms. But it had only been a few weeks. *Love?* It felt right, but it still terrified Lettie. Love made you do wacky things, things like blow up your town and write notebooks full of embarrassing poetry.

"Sorry, I don't mean to freak you out," Chandler said, "and you don't have to say it back. You really don't. But, for me, yeah, I love you. I loved you when I was eighteen and it scared the shit out of me. And it's not like I've spent the last decade pining for you, but I never found that again."

"You loved me?" Lettie had certainly thought she had been in love with Chandler, but she'd never said it, never even come close, though their summer together had been so good before it went so wrong.

"Yeah, of course I loved you, Lettie. I loved you so much it made the earth explode. I thought you knew." She stroked her fingers down Lettie's arm and onto her bare back, where she flattened her palm and held her tight. "So, I know what it feels like."

"I'm…" She sighed.

"Forgiveness is enough," Chandler said, "I just wanted you to know."

They laid in silence for a while; the tv playing quietly in the background. Love. It was a big word. Lettie kissed Chandler's chest through her shirt and ran her hand up Chandler's stomach. She could feel the beat of her heart, feel the dark magic inside of her reaching its tendrils towards Lettie. But now it didn't feel so dark, simply different. A magic not her own, but one that called to her, that longed for her.

"We did what we said we were going to do, scare the shit out of Alvin. I'm not sure it worked."

"It was always a flimsy plan," Chandler said. "But the story is supposed to run tomorrow. And if that doesn't work it's okay. It was my mistake. And I'm an adult, it's time for me to accept some consequences. So, if I'm out a couple thousand dollars, then I'm out a couple thousand dollars. It's not like I have rent to pay. But after what happened today, I don't want him here anymore. I want him gone, and I don't want you worried about the Lodge, so I'm going to make sure that happens. I just want us."

"I'm really glad you came back," Lettie said. Before Chandler had shown up, she'd imagined their reunion many times, more in the earlier years and less recently. Never would she have thought it ended like this, wrapped in her arms, Chandler making promises Lettie actually believed she'd keep. "I always thought you found me annoying."

"Oh, I did." There was laughter in Chandler's voice. "But in an endearing way. You were the golden child around Lilac Lake. When I was little, I didn't understand that it wasn't because the rest of us were lacking, it was just because you were spectacular."

"What changed?" Lettie worried she would regret hearing the answer.

"Puberty." And Lettie didn't need to see Chandler's face to know she was smirking. "You started wearing those little bikinis at the lake. I had to rethink a couple of things."

"Shut up."

"I'm just answering the question."

Lettie pushed herself up and crawled up Chandler's chest, kissing her slowly, deliberately. "A bikini, huh?"

"Oh, I'm really looking forward to summer, Ms. Katz." She pushed a strand of strawberry blonde hair behind Lettie's ear. "It might be my favorite season."

Lettie could feel the tension coming off Chandler. She could also see it—wisps of dark, smokey magic danced around her before changing into snowy flakes of stone they would need to sweep up later.

"You look fine," Lettie said, watching her brush mascara across her eyelashes.

"Okay." She adjusted her septum ring then adjusted it again. "Why am I so nervous?"

"I don't know. But it's cute." It was. Chandler rarely looked frazzled.

She rolled up the sleeves of her button-up, revealing muscled arms and dark tattoos. "What if I hit him too?"

"Don't." Lettie stepped closer, and her magic perked up at the proximity to Chandler. "No hitting. Only light threatening. Dinner after?"

"Or…" Chandler walked her fingers up Lettie's arm. "We could stay in. Celebrate the nullification of my contract. The end of my dumbassery." She cupped Lettie's chin and ran her thumb along her lips. "Champagne. Candlelight."

"I think I could be persuaded." Lettie pressed her thighs together because they had places to be. She reached up, straightening Chandler's tie, and maybe giving it a little extra tug.

Chandler looked down at her, pulling her bottom lip between her teeth. "Later," she said breathlessly. "Later."

Outside, the sun had returned, but the temperature continued to drop, and the air smelled like snow. It was still early in the year, probably too early, but Lettie let herself hope. It didn't snow often in Lilac Lake, but when it did it was beautiful.

They headed towards town, holding hands. Monica had assured them Alvin was renting the apartment above the coffee shop. Lettie hoped she was correct because she didn't want to have to track him down.

As they approached his apartment, Lettie gave Chandler's hand a squeeze. Neither of them spoke, but Chandler returned the squeeze, her shoulders squared and her eyes straight ahead.

When they got there, Chandler paused and inhaled. "I swore I'd never be back here, now I'm fighting to stay."

The words should sting, but they didn't. Lettie was proud of Chandler. She knew how hard it was to grow, to embrace the parts of yourself that frightened you.

Chandler shook out her hands and pushed up her sleeves. "Okay, I'm ready."

"Wait." Lettie stepped in front of Chandler and looked her over, deep green eyes, high cheekbones, beautiful dark hair falling in curls. "I'm proud of you." She kissed her, a quick peck, then stepped back. "Whatever happens, you've got this."

They went around the coffee shop to the stairs in the back. The landing was full of potted plants that Lettie was sure looked gorgeous in spring, but currently just looked brown. The wooden deck had been swept recently and everything was just so. She imagined Alvin Condon out on the landing, broom in hand.

He must be a meticulous man in his everyday life. His suits were always pressed, his hair neatly done. For him it must be awful being in

Lilac Lake, surrounded by unpredictable people; people who ate fried chicken with their hands and grew wildflowers instead of lawns. People who had never been in a boardroom and spent their afternoons in tubes on the lake getting sunburnt.

Chandler knocked three swift raps on the door. They could hear footsteps inside, then the door swung open. Alvin's shirt was only partially buttoned and untucked. No tie, no jacket. He blinked at them and then frowned, his forehead creasing. "Hello?"

"Can we come in? No magic," Chandler said, holding her hands up as if to prove nothing would be turned to stone.

He squinted at them, and his forehead remained creased. Then he nodded. "Come in."

Inside the apartment was small and sparsely decorated, but immaculately clean. Nothing like the cluttered, knickknack laden spaces that both Lettie and Chandler lived in.

"Would you like some tea," he asked, his voice laced with suspicion.

"No, thank you," Chandler said.

"Have a seat." He gestured to the couch, and both women sat. He sat across from them in a slim armchair, one leg crossed over the other.

"I'd like to talk to you about the contract."

In an instant his entire demeanor changed, his forehead smoothed, and a smile toyed with the edges of his mouth. The sudden change made Lettie's stomach turn. She nearly grabbed Chandler. Nothing that made Alvin Condon look so happy could be good for them.

"Yes, I've had some thoughts on that as well. One moment." He slapped his hands on his thighs and stood up.

Lettie glanced at Chandler, but the space was small, there was nothing she could whisper that wouldn't be overheard, and besides he was back in seconds. He put a manilla folder down on the coffee table but didn't open it. "I do not think a professional relationship between my company and Ms. Katz is going to work."

Lettie clamped her jaw shut so tightly her teeth hurt. She knew there was more coming before he said it. He was too happy, nearly smirking. Beside her she could feel Chandler's magic, as though it reached out to her, touching her when Chandler couldn't. A glance towards her confirmed Lettie's suspicions, her eyes were stony, hard as rock.

Well, fuck this man, and fuck professionalism. Lettie reached into the space between them, taking Chandler's hand. She caressed her, trying to soothe the tension she could feel building, and stroking her thumb over the veins on the back of Chandler's hand.

He glanced down at their hands and then back up. "Of course, this town is a marvelous location, ripe for expansion. Our contract would be a conflict of interest. You'll be thrilled to learn I called the firm this morning. I'm taking a step back at work, focusing more on my true passion, hospitality. A friend will be joining me soon, we plan to buy up some land and turn Lilac Lake into the tourism hub it was always meant to be."

Lettie felt like she was listening to a villain describe his malignant plans, except she was no heroine, and she had no sword to run him through with.

"So, you'll be giving me the money then," Chandler said through gritted teeth.

Alvin chuckled. "You're free to pursue that if you would like. Just as I'm sure Hillchamp is free to represent you in court. But as I said, I am stepping away. If the contract cannot be amicably dissolved, there are others from the firm willing to step in."

Chandler's magic spiked, a fiery spark against Lettie's palm that almost made her jump. Lettie squeezed Chandler's hand in response. The man was an annoying little shit, but this was what they had wanted, at least this part of it. The contract would be void, Chandler would have the Stone and Sorcery Lodge.

She turned in her seat to look at Chandler. "Don't take the bait." And she didn't care if Alvin Condon heard her. She wanted him to know what a sleaze she thought he was. "There's nowhere for him to build a hotel. He's not our problem."

For a moment, Lettie thought Chandler was going to launch out of her seat and throttle him, but she nodded. "Of course." She turned back towards Alvin. "You have it drawn up already? I'd like to have my lawyer look at it."

Again, he laughed, and again the urge to run him through with a sword gripped Lettie. "Really?"

"Yes." Chandler swiped the folder off the table and opened the papers, thumbing through them. "I will return them once they're signed."

"Excellent." Alvin stood up. "Say, do you know any good realtors? This place is lovely, but I'd like something with a yard."

There it was again, the murderous rage. "You're never going to find a home here," Lettie said.

"Well, there's that southern hospitality I've heard so much about. I'm really looking forward to your festival, Lettie. Should bring in sizeable crowds."

The folder in Chandler's hand flickered, stone then back to paper. Lettie threaded her arm through Chandler's and yanked her toward the doorway before Alvin Condon became a statue.

She pushed the door shut behind them and hurried down the stairs until they were on the other side of the coffee shop.

"I want to strangle him," Chandler said, gripping the folder with white knuckles. The papers were going to be a crumpled mess by the time they were returned.

"That makes two of us." Lettie glanced up at the apartment over the shop. "He can't really get land here, can he?"

"Who knows? He's a son of a bitch, trust fund, nepotism shit bag!" Chandler yelled the last words up at his apartment. "And what can't a shit bag get in America?"

"Let's take a walk," Lettie said.

The town was mostly deserted, tourists were gone, and townies were at work. But the sun was bright despite the chill in the air, and cottony clouds floated across the sky. Lilac Lake was beautiful, even in winter, and a walk would do them both good, even if it only served to put distance between them and Alvin.

For a while, the two of them were silent. Visions of homicide danced in Lettie's head, making her magic come to life inside of her— apparently her magic loved violence.

"I think I want to go punch him. Yeah, I definitely want to punch him." Chandler turned on her heel.

Lettie scrambled to grab her, pulling her by the arm. There were no words to calm Chandler, so instead she kissed her, crashing their mouths together and grasping a handful of her hair.

Her magic raged against Lettie, but her mouth opened, her tongue sweeping through Lettie's mouth and her hands grasped her sides, fingers digging into Lettie's skin until it hurt.

Chandler shoved her thigh between Lettie's legs, pushing her back into the building behind them. She moved her mouth to Lettie's neck, her hands making their way under Lettie's shirt and then she broke away gasping. "Fuck."

Lettie's chest heaved, and she yearned to pull Chandler back to her. "Let's drop those off at Hillchamp's, quickly, okay?"

"Yeah, okay."

-CHAPTER TWENTY-FIVE-

THE CABINS WERE finished. The contractor had put in the last of the flooring that morning, and now they stood empty, but full of promise. Two weeks had passed since Chandler had signed the paperwork. The Stone and Sorcery Lodge was owned, as it was always meant to be, by a Hart and a Katz.

Unfortunately, during those two weeks Alvin had moved into one of the little brick ranch houses a few miles from town center. Lettie had heard through the grapevine, aka Monica and Ginger, that he'd wanted one of the older homes along Main Street, one of which was for sale, and another for rent, and been refused on both accounts.

Lettie sipped her coffee then tiptoed towards the bedroom. They were supposed to meet the contractor in an hour, but Chandler was still in bed, naked and bathed in sunlight, her dark hair a frizzy halo around her head.

Lettie put her mug on the dresser and crawled into bed beside her. She started her kisses at Chandler's abdomen and worked up, circling her tongue around one of her nipples then moving to her neck, her cheek. "Good morning," she whispered in her ear.

"Keep going," Chandler moaned without opening her eyes. "Back down. Lower."

Lettie obeyed, lowering her mouth, swirling her tongue over Chandler's skin. When she got to her thighs, she pushed herself up and Chandler opened her eyes. "Good morning," Lettie smiled. "Did you know…" She kissed Chandler's thighs, one then the other. "That I love you?"

"Yeah?" Chandler smiled, her eyes still soft with sleep. "I love you too. Come here."

"There?" Lettie retreated back between Chandler's thighs, running her tongue up the center of her. She looked up, replacing her mouth with her thumb, sliding it, too softly, over Chandler's clit. "Not here?"

Chandler's head was thrown back, her spine just beginning to arch off the bed. She reached down, tangling her fingers in Lettie's hair, forcing her back down between her thighs.

She held Lettie in place as she ground her core against her, making Lettie ache with her own want as she moved her tongue against Chandler's slick center.

Lettie ran a finger through her wetness and then pushed it inside of her. Chandler made a delicious little noise, tightening around her. "You taste good," Lettie whispered against her skin before returning her mouth to Chandler.

She couldn't believe she could have months, years, decades of this. Of this beautiful, strange, complicated woman. She pressed another finger into her, tightening the circling of her tongue.

Chandler came quickly, still drowsy with sleep and making small little whimpering noises instead of her usual roar and Lettie was all the wetter for it.

But she recovered quickly as her body stilled. She let go of Lettie and pushed herself up on her forearms. "Stand up and take off your clothes. Now."

"Or?" Lettie teased.

"Or I'm not going to fuck you before we go to our meeting," she said. She watched Lettie as she stood, pulling off her clothes. Chandler put her hand between her thighs, touching herself as Lettie undressed, her eyes hot and fierce.

Lettie watched her hungrily as she removed her pants and then her underwear. She longed to replace Chandler's hand with her own, to touch her, make her squirm again.

"Sit at the vanity," Chandler said, and Lettie obeyed that too, easing herself onto the soft cushioned seat and spreading her thighs, her stomach clenching as Chandler's eyes followed.

Chandler stood, prowling across the bedroom and knelt between Lettie's legs. She gripped Lettie by the waist, then ran her hands up, gripping Lettie's breasts. She pulled one of her nipples into her mouth, swirling her tongue against the sensitive skin.

But Lettie wanted her touch, wanted Chandler's hands where she throbbed. Instead, Chandler moved back, and looked up at Lettie, a devious smirk on her face. "Turn around, on your knees."

"What?"

"Watch me fuck you," she said, running her hands up Lettie's legs, gripping her thigh for a moment before scooting back.

Heart pounding, Lettie turned around, gripping the edge of the vanity, her knees digging into the seat.

Chandler spread her open and ran her fingers down Lettie's wet, throbbing center, all while Lettie watched in the mirror, watched Chandler's eyes blaze with desire and she lowered her mouth to Lettie who had never felt more bare, more open.

"I love you," she gasped out as Chandler's tongue made its first swipe of her clit. "I love you," she repeated as Chandler grasped her with both hands, pulling her closer to her.

She ate Lettie's pussy as though she was starving, reaching up to grasp one of her breasts, her other hand still holding Lettie tightly. And all Lettie could do was grasp the wood of the vanity as her world narrowed to a pinprick, just the space between her legs where Chandler's tongue ran.

Her whole body turned tight like wound coils and then, just as suddenly, she released with a scream, nearly collapsing as her legs shook and her muscles contracted. When she finished shaking, Chandler stood, pulling Lettie with her.

"Open your eyes," Chandler said.

Lettie hadn't realized she had closed them, but she did. In the mirror her cheeks were flushed, and Chandler was beautiful, even with wild morning hair and heavy-lidded eyes. Lettie turned in her arms and kissed her fiercely, pressing their naked bodies together. "You are mine," she said.

"Yes, I am. Forever."

When they finally made their way out of the bedroom, Oak was waiting for them in the dining room with Daphne. Lettie wasn't sure when the two of them had become friends, but they were both laughing when she got there.

"They wanted to see, too," Daphne said, standing up and brushing crumbs off her dress. She always looked right in winter, like she belonged, an ice princess from another time. Before Lettie had ever met a fae she'd imagined them like Daphne's family, lithe and long-haired. She'd still only met a handful, and sometimes that's still how she pictured them in her mind.

"We'll need a groundskeeper," Lettie said. She knew Oak had a green thumb; she'd seen their family gardens. "Know anyone interested?"

Oak smiled, lighting up their face. "Are you offering me a job? I never thought I'd see the day."

"You've thought of this day?" Lettie wasn't sure how to respond.

"Oh, I've dreamed of Chandler becoming a productive member of society for my whole life," they teased.

"Are you sure the two of you don't want to get a first look at your hard work alone?" Daphne asked. "Oak and I could get brunch, meet you after."

"It's hardly just our hard work," Lettie said, moving closer to Chandler. "And we want you there."

"Then we're happy to oblige," Daphne said, leading the way.

The four of them headed towards the cabins, moving closer to each other as the freezing wind whipped around them. The leaves had given up the fight and the last stragglers littered the ground, crunching under their feet.

"What do you think he's going to do next?" Chandler asked, voicing the question that had plagued Lettie.

What *did* Alvin have planned? Was he really going to move into Lilac Lake and build a hotel? But while the question rattled around in her brain, the fear behind it was miniscule.

"Who cares. We'll figure it out," Lettie said. She was done being afraid of him, done worrying what he would do. Whatever happened, staying up all night thinking about it wouldn't change anything. And she was proud of the Stone and Sorcery. She believed in its ability to withstand whatever came next.

And she also believed in the town, that it was more than a tourist trap. Lilac Lake was her home and now it was Chandler's too. Their roots went deep into the soil, and Lettie planned to flourish in it, build something strong.

The lake sparkled like diamonds in the winter sun, small waves kicking up along the rocky shore.

The four of them paused as the cabins came into view, each of them freshly painted a gorgeous green that matched the lake behind them. Their walkways were a sharp contrast against the brown grass, beautiful, patterned marble that had yet to be walked on.

"You need to get a photographer out here," Daphne said. "You'll be booked in minutes. This looks amazing."

Lettie could picture it, the firepit that sat in the middle burning, people laughing and drinking beers, children splashing in the water. She reached down and threaded her fingers through Chandler's.

"We did it," Chandler whispered, nuzzling against her neck briefly.

"We really did," Lettie said. She walked up the pathway to the nearest cabin and pushed open the door.

Chandler flipped on the light, and Lettie's heart swelled. Inside the cabin was a symphony of beautiful, soft colors, inviting couches, and soft chairs.

The others followed her in, and Daphne ran her fingers around the mantle. Lorne had intricately carved the wood with swirling shapes and Lilac petals. He'd custom-built coffee tables for each cabin with burned wood and legs that matched the mantle.

It was warm and inviting yet refined. She wished their grandmothers could see it. They'd always talked about redoing the cabins, and she knew they'd be proud. She hoped they'd be proud of her and Chandler for so many other things too.

"We should go get some beer. Spend the night here," Daphne said, turning in a slow circle as she took in all the details of the cabin. "A little sleepover."

Chandler wrapped her arms around Lettie's waist and rested her head on her shoulder. "That would be perfect."

-TWO MONTHS LATER-

LETTIE'S PHONE DINGED on the side table, but she didn't need to look to know it was Amelia. She'd been messaging her pretty much nonstop for the last week. The festival was still months away and so far, almost nothing had gone wrong, but that hadn't stopped her from worrying.

Lettie left the message unread and unanswered. She had other things on her mind. She looked herself over in the mirror. The curls in her hair were holding up, and her make-up wasn't smudged. She smoothed the lines of her dress one last time and nodded at her reflection, satisfied with the result.

The bedroom door clicked open, and Lettie turned. Chandler looked gorgeous. Her dark curls were loose around her face, her eyeliner sharp, and her green eyes bright. She had on a pair of skintight leather pants and a low-cut blouse that made Lettie reconsider leaving for their date as she eyed the soft curve of her breasts.

Lettie walked across the room and ran her hands down Chandler's sides, dragging her thumbs across her hip bones, and Chandler pulled her close.

"You look delicious."

Chandler's magic was still a dark, twisting thing, but it warmed Lettie, and her own magic responded, green tendrils dancing around them. No longer did fear lace her power, it was hers, an extension of her will, her desire.

Lettie kissed Chandler slowly, only pulling back to drag her teeth along Chandler's bottom lip. They had a date tonight, something they tried to do every week, but would probably have to miss as the seasons changed and the Lodge increased its occupancy.

This week they were leaving Lilac Lake, driving a few towns over to an Italian restaurant Lettie had always wanted to try but had never been to.

Chandler's fingers moved from Lettie's hips to the bottom of her dress. She pushed up the fabric and ran her hands along Lettie's thighs. "I love you, beautiful."

"I love you, too," Lettie murmured against the smooth skin of her neck as she planted kisses along Chandler's throat.

And she did. Though it had taken her longer than Chandler to fully fall, she'd known the path she was on from the first moment she'd seen her at Hillchamp's office. Though love took more trust than lust

Chandler had earned it with each passing day; a growing faith that built on itself.

"We should go," Lettie said, because if they stayed, she was going to drag Chandler to the bed and not leave for a very long time.

"Okay, okay. Fine." Chandler stepped away, letting her hands linger for a moment longer, then took Lettie's hand in her own.

Outside of their apartments, the Lodge was starting to come alive as winter made its first concessions to spring. They'd had the rooms painted, the floor refinished, and updated the furniture. Once she had updated the pictures on their website, they'd been almost fully booked by the end of the day.

As for Alvin, he was around. She saw him sometimes, scowling in town square, or typing away on his phone over a cup of coffee. But so far, she hadn't heard anything about him buying land. She was sure something would happen eventually, but she brushed it off. Right now, she and Chandler were happy, still learning about each other, finding all the ways they had changed over the last eleven years.

Chandler held the door for her and then re-intertwined their fingers. "Do you really think Oak is going to run for mayor?" she asked, heading for her car.

Lettie shrugged. "I hope so. This town could use a little shaking up."

Daphne and Oak's story is coming soon. Sign up for my newsletter at www.tallierose.com to stay updated.

More books by Tallie Rose:

Sapphic Vampire Retellings

Hecate's Hollow

Calla Falling

Briar Constance Series

As Played by Gods

An Echo of Gods

Sympathy for the Gods (Coming soon)

Sea and Flame Series

Sea and Flame

Scale and Smoke

www.ingramcontent.com/pod-product-compliance
Lightning Source LLC
Chambersburg PA
CBHW051142130726
47988CB00005B/1957